There was a
woman se...

"Dace Recker," he said by way of introduction. "Have you made contact with the hostage taker yet?"

Her back was to him, but he heard her say, "Hello. To whom am I speaking?"

His heart stuttered in his chest. The voice was familiar. Too familiar. It still haunted his dreams. Prowled his subconscious. Summoned memories he'd done his damnedest to forget for the past year and a half. Desperately he raked her figure with his gaze, seeking a sign that he was wrong.

But a moment later she swung around to face him and recognition struck him square in the chest. No matter how impossible it seemed, how cruel, it *was* Jolie Conrad. The only woman he'd ever allowed close enough to get a grip on his heart.

The same woman who'd ripped that organ out of his chest when she'd walked out of his life eighteen months ago, after their world had shattered around them.

Dear Reader,

Most officers on SWAT teams have call signs, code names they use to refer to each other. And rarely are they derived from a particularly dazzling display of brilliance ☺. Rather, one mishap earns an officer a witty call sign that will be a constant reminder of his or her miscalculation. Given some of my own less than brainy moves, I shudder to think what call sign I'd be saddled with!

I first got the idea for this series from watching a TV show about a pair of hostage negotiators who were romantically involved. But as I researched SWAT, I became intrigued by the other teams making up the unit, as well: tactical entry, command center, hostage rescue, sniper. I was awed by the heroism these men and women display, putting their lives on the line every day for complete strangers. Doing their part to keep our world a little safer.

The characters of ALPHA SQUAD were born from that research and admiration. Brave, daring and flawed, each of them faces danger with unflinching courage. But they all have life lessons to learn when it comes to dealing with the greatest risk of all—falling in love.

I hope you enjoy their journeys as much as I enjoyed writing them!

All the best,

Kylie Brant

Terms of
SURRENDER
Kylie Brant

Silhouette®
Romantic
SUSPENSE

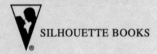

SILHOUETTE BOOKS

ISBN-13: 978-0-373-27603-5
ISBN-10:   0-373-27603-6

TERMS OF SURRENDER

Copyright © 2008 by Kimberly Bahnsen

Books by Kylie Brant

Silhouette Romantic Suspense

*The Sullivan Brothers
†Charmed and Dangerous
**The Tremaine Tradition
††Alpha Squad

KYLIE BRANT

is the award-winning author of more than twenty novels. When she's not dreaming up stories of romance and suspense, she works as an elementary teacher for learning disabled students. Kylie has dealt with her newly empty nest by filling the house with even more books, and won't be satisfied until those five vacant bedrooms are full of them!

Kylie invites readers to check out her Web site at www.kyliebrant.com. You can contact her by writing to P.O. Box 231, Charles City, IA 50616, or e-mailing her at kyliebrant@hotmail.com.

For Kasen James, my precious second grandson,
whose smiles light up my heart.

Acknowledgments

A special thanks to Mark Pfeiffer and Jeff McQueen,
weapons experts at Weapons_Info loop, for the wealth
of knowledge you share every day, and for that final clue
that tied my plot together. You guys are amazing!
And a big thank-you to my experts on hostage
negotiation and SWAT: Jay Chase and Jerry MacCauley,
director of Personal Protection Concepts, for your
patience answering questions and helping me understand
the basics; Sgt. Michael Fanning (ret.), NYPD Hostage
Negotiation Team, for walking through my plot with me
to get the details right; and Kyle Hiller, Captain, Special
Response Team, for your generosity of time, detailed
explanations and invaluable assistance. You're my heroes,
every one of you!

Chapter 1

Dace Recker donned the Tac-Vest with its heavy ceramic plates and fastened it. Grabbing his bag of gear out of the car's trunk, he slammed the lid and jogged toward the police tape establishing the outer perimeter around the bank. Ducking beneath it, he flashed his shield at the cop stationed nearest him and began to shoulder his way through the sea of law enforcement officers toward the Negotiations Operation Center, a converted ambulance, parked nearby.

"Dace!" Turning, he recognized Jack Langley from Alpha Squad, the SWAT unit his Hostage Negotiation Team was assigned to. Jack's limp was noticeable in his hurry. The injury he'd sustained in the explosion at the Metrodome last month still had him on the disabled list. At that moment, however, HNT leader, Bradley Lewis, stepped out of the NOC mobile unit and spotted Dace, waving him over. Jack caught up with him as he headed toward Lewis and said urgently, "Your new partner's here."

"Yeah?" Dace craned his neck, but could see no one standing near the commander. "Who is it? Have you met him yet?"

"Her. And she's—"

"Recker, where the hell is your team responding from, Siberia?"

Lewis's familiar impatient tone succeeded in snapping Dace's attention from Langley.

"What's the situation?"

"Bank branch with twelve regular employees, ten of them confirmed inside. Undetermined number of customers, but witnesses suggest at least eight. Someone managed to press the crisis button, which alerted police at 9:21 a.m. Subject went barricade shortly after."

Dace checked his watch. 10:12.

"Shots fired upon entry, and again fifteen minutes later," Lewis continued. "No visual yet. The blinds were pulled shortly after the first shots were fired."

"Injuries?"

"Nothing confirmed. The situation's locked down with a full perimeter established. Your new partner's inside the mobile unit, trying to establish contact. You'll be primary, but she's got plenty of experience, too. The phone lines have been disconnected. The gunman did accept the throw phone, but hasn't answered it yet."

Dace nodded as Lewis turned and strode toward the command center, a sleek black specially equipped RV. The man would serve as their command center liaison, exchanging information with the SWAT commander. As Dace reached for the door to the NOC unit, his progress was halted by Jack's hand on his arm.

"Like I was saying…"

"A woman partner. Yeah, I heard you. Eat your heart out, buddy." Dace shot a grin at his friend. "When you get back on duty, all you have to look forward to is Bazuk." The eerily silent tobacco-chewing Cajun was Jack's personal nemesis, primarily, Dace figured, because both men had more than their share of ego.

But Langley didn't take the bait. "Yeah, yeah, but there's something you should know. I saw her when I was in human resources filling out insurance stuff."

"Who, the new partner?"

"Yeah, and it's—"

"Langley!"

Dace hid a grin at the sound of SWAT commander Harv Mendel's familiar bellow from the command center parked a hundred yards away. As Langley turned in resignation, Dace opened the back door of the NOC unit and ducked inside. Mendel was going to want to know what the man was doing on-site when he hadn't yet gotten a medical release to return to duty. But Dace knew his friend well enough to figure the answer. With nothing to do but rehab exercises, Langley was going slowly crazy. A civilian might spend his medical leave at the beach. Jack spent his listening to the scanner.

The unit was nearly empty save for a slender blond woman, seated at the table. Most of the team must not have arrived yet. "Dace Recker," he said by way of introduction. "Have you made contact yet?"

Her back was to him, but he heard her say, "Hello. Whom am I speaking to?"

His heart stuttered in his chest. The voice was familiar. Too familiar. It still haunted his dreams. Prowled his subconscious. Summoned memories he'd done his damnedest to forget for the past year and a half.

Disbelieving, he raked her figure with his gaze, desperately seeking a sign that he was wrong. This woman was slimmer, wasn't she? Her hair a lighter shade than he remembered.

But a moment later she swung around to face him and recognition struck him square in the chest. No matter how impossible it seemed, how cruel, it *was* Jolie Conrad. The only woman he'd ever allowed close enough to get a grip on his heart.

The same woman who'd ripped that organ out of his chest when she'd walked out of his life eighteen months ago, after their world had shattered around them.

Her expression mirrored his shock. But she recovered first, holding out the cell. "Out of seven calls made, this is the first answered. Woman's voice. She's handing it over to the gunman."

He took the phone she extended as if it were a lifeline. Speaking with the psycho inside the bank who was holding at least eighteen hostages was infinitely preferable to dealing with the emotional punch of seeing Jolie again.

Not just seeing her. Being partnered with her.

God help him.

"This is Dace Recker, with the Metro City Police Department." It took more effort than it should have to keep his focus on the hostage taker at the other end of the line. "Am I speaking to the person in charge?"

"You are. And I have to say, Recker, that you and your people are screwing up my day."

The voice was male. Authoritative. Native English speaker. No trace of regional accents. Dace's assessments were instinctive, made in quick succession.

He glanced at his partner. *Jolie.* His gut tightened. She'd donned earphones and was listening intently to the conversation. "I'm here to give you a hand with that…" Deliberately he let his voice trail off. "Help me out, here. What's your name?"

"Names aren't important."

He kept his voice easy. "Well, they sort of are. I have to call you something, don't I?"

There was a moment's hesitation. "Just call me John."

"All right, John, talk to me. Are you all right?"

The question seemed to catch the other man off guard. "I'm fine."

"That's good. I'm very glad to hear that. I want to keep it that way, okay, John? How about the rest of the folks in there? Are there any injuries?"

"You don't seem to understand how things are going to work, so let me explain. I want a black SUV with tinted windows delivered to the back doors. Pull your perimeter back another six hundred yards. Too many cops around here. I'm feeling a little claustrophobic."

"I'll work on it. No one's coming in there, John, but we're not going anywhere either. Now this is a two-way effort. You want something, you have to give something in return. I really need the status on the people inside with you. How many are there? Are there any in need of medical assistance?"

"There's one past need of medical assistance," came the chilling reply. "And there will be more if you don't follow my directions exactly." The line abruptly disconnected.

Releasing a breath, he set the phone down. Only then did he transfer his attention to Lewis, who had entered the unit and slipped on headphones during the conversation. "Did you get that?"

Lewis took off his headphones and headed for the door. "I'll run the delivery-exchange angle by command center. If he reestablishes contact before I return, you know the drill."

Dace did know it. Stall him. Establish a rapport by using

active listening skills. Once command center okayed it, the team would work an exchange while getting concessions for the people inside. Releasing the injured. Sending in food. But this was the trickiest part of negotiation. He didn't know the gunman well enough yet to predict how he was going to react when Dace followed the usual procedures.

He slanted a glance to the woman at his side, who even now was looking at him, her blue eyes guarded. And he knew this case had been complicated beyond all measure the moment he'd heard her voice and come face-to-face with the past that still plagued him.

The open back door framed Dr. Ryder, their psychological profiler, who'd stopped to talk to Lewis for a moment. With an effort at keeping their privacy, Jolie spoke in a whisper. "I'm sorry about this."

His loins tightened, as if in conditioned response to that familiar smoky tone. He gave her a grim smile and lowered his voice, too. "For what? Sucker punching me with this partnership? For not returning my phone calls? Or for taking off without a word a year and a half ago and leaving me to wonder what the hell had happened to you?" He could hear the bitterness lacing his words, but was helpless to temper it. "Take your pick, Jolie. What are you apologizing for? For walking out of my life? Or for walking back into it?"

Jolie's palms were damp, but she refused to show weakness in front of this man by wiping them on her pants. Meeting Dace's condemning green gaze took a strength of will that sapped her system. She'd been as dismayed as he when she'd looked up to see him in the doorway. Perhaps she shouldn't have been surprised. There were only two SWAT/HNT squads in Metro City. And if she'd learned nothing else in her life, it was that fate was filled with the cruelest of ironies.

"When I was placed back on HNT, I never dreamed I'd be

partnered with you. I'd heard you quit the squad after…" Her voice faltered as his gaze sharpened. She didn't want him to think she'd been checking up on him. But occasionally touching base with old friends on the force had invariably included department gossip.

"After you left? Yeah, I quit the squad for a while. Rejoined last January." He studied her a moment, an impassive expression on his face. "When did you come back? And why?"

His words were sharp as a blade. He was equally adept at wielding them like a weapon, she recalled. Slicing through subterfuge and carving at defenses until emotion, raw and unvarnished, leaked out. Until she said things she wished she could retract. Did things she still regretted.

"A month ago." Answering the second half of his question would take more time than they had. And far more openness on her part than she'd ever granted before. Since he didn't even know her mother existed, it'd be a little difficult to explain returning to Metro City to care for her.

He gave her a humorless smile. "A month. Great." He turned away abruptly to address the other team members who had gathered outside. And she was left with the crushing certainty that she'd added another royal screwup to the mess her life had always been. It was useless to wonder how to fix it. If she'd had any success in that area, she wouldn't be here.

So she did the one thing she could do. Focused on the only part of her life that was black-and-white. The only part she'd ever shown an ounce of aptitude for.

She turned her focus to the SWAT incident report and began filling in the necessary information. Because every second she concentrated on the job was another second she didn't have to think about the man beside her. Didn't have to face the pain she'd caused him. The pain they'd caused each other.

Minutes later the newcomers entered the NOC, each taking a place around the table, filling the cramped quarters.

Dace made introductions. "Dr. Phil Ryder, our profiler." A stocky man with a shiny balding pate gave her a nod. "Lance Sharper will be recorder and Herb Johnson tactical liaison." He indicated each of the individuals in turn and inclined his head toward Jolie. "Jolie Conrad, new to the squad but not to HNT."

"Any problems with the throw phone?" Johnson wanted to know.

"For once we actually had enough cord, believe it or not," Dace replied. It was never a matter of *if* things went wrong on a SWAT response, it was a matter of *when*. There were invariably screwups, like equipment that didn't work or throw phones that didn't have long enough cords to reach the barricaded subject.

While Dace brought the other members up-to-date, Jolie got up to maneuver around the table and jot notes on the white marker board that lined the walls of the unit. It would serve as their situation board, and as circumstances unfolded they would make copious notes of every communication with the hostage taker, as well as impressions formed during the conversations. It was crucial that every piece of information be documented to aid in drawing conclusions. The profiler would weigh the HT's words carefully before rendering an impression about how best to approach the subject.

The door opened and Lewis ducked his head to enter, a roll of papers under his arm. Flicking his gaze over the assembled group, he grunted. "Good. You're all here."

The command center liaison sat in the empty chair and unrolled the plans on the table. The rest of the team members crowded around.

"No basement," Jolie observed. "One level simplifies things."

"If the squad has to infiltrate, yeah." Dace's voice was impersonal, as if their earlier exchange had never occurred. Jolie knew she could count on him to compartmentalize their past and focus on the task at hand. He could be as single-minded on the job as she.

"But it's also easier for the hostage taker to control the hostages," Dr. Ryder pointed out. "Fewer places for them to scatter."

They examined the blueprints as a voice crackled in Johnson's headset. The whipcord-thin black man listened for a moment before stating, "Intel reports no live subjects in sight at this time. The body looks like a security guard. The rest of the lobby floor is littered with clothes and shoes."

"How much?" Jolie put in, her mind racing.

"Piles of them."

"He made them undress," she said and saw Dace nod. "He's been planning this for a while. Figured out the best way to control a group of people was to strip them, figuratively and literally, of all outer trappings of position."

"And keep them preoccupied with more basic issues than escape," Ryder put in.

If that were the strategy, it would be crudely effective. But, more important, it gave them critical details about the gunman they were dealing with. His choice of words, during the short time they'd had him on the phone, had depicted a man of some education. Unless he'd had a sexual motive for stripping his hostages—which Jolie doubted—they now knew the gunman had an underlying understanding of basic human nature and how to manipulate it.

Which meant he might be smart enough to see through attempts to manipulate him, as well.

Sharper traced the blueprint with a blunt-edged finger. "He'll keep them all together. Only places available would

be a restroom—tight fit for all those people—these two
offices or the vault." He reached up to wipe his broad forehead. The air-conditioning in the NOC unit was notoriously
unreliable.

Jolie studied the diagram more closely. The vault would
be the obvious choice, since it would allow the greatest
security, and give the HT a way to lock the hostages inside.
But was there room? It was a sizable space, but she had to
assume the money and bonds that a bank kept on hand would
take up a great deal of that room.

"Any hope for witness identification on the gunman?"

Lewis shook his head in response to Dace's question. "Not
yet. The good news is that the security video streams to an
outside company, so we should be able to clearly see all the customers and employees walking into the bank. Mendel is waiting
for the feed now. He's got it figured as a robbery gone bad."

It was the most obvious motivation, but Jolie had learned
never to assume anything in these situations. It could just as
easily be a disgruntled former employee. Or someone who'd
been turned down for a loan, or one with any number of
grudges against someone inside.

Dr. Ryder turned to study the notes Jolie had jotted down.
Dace got up to attach the blueprints to the situation board with
magnets. The team debated the best approach to take in the
next conversation.

Several minutes later, they reached consensus. "Then we're
agreed," Lewis said, sending a look around the table. "We play
to the HT's need for control while we work the exchange angle."

"You might want to see if he responds differently to Jolie,"
Dr. Ryder suggested. "It's early enough in the process that a
rapport hasn't been established yet. And if he's as driven by
control as we think, he may believe a female is easier to
manage."

Dace shrugged. "Try him again. See what he'll give up."

Jolie nodded, already pressing Redial. Concessions were a staple of hostage negotiation. Nothing was ever given to a suspect without law enforcement getting something in return. In one situation she'd worked, the gunman had exchanged two hostages for a carton of cigarettes.

The ringing stopped as the call connected. "John? This is Jolie Conrad, with the Metro PD. We've passed your requests on. But we need you to do something for us—"

"What happened to Recker?"

She slid a gaze to Dace, listening at her side. "He's here, John. Do you want to speak to him?"

Indifference sounded in the man's voice. "It doesn't matter. How long before I get that SUV?"

"Like I said, the arrangements are in the works. But you have to give us something, too. Life is a series of compromises, right?" She could almost feel the green intensity of Dace's eyes boring into her. Too late, she recalled how often she'd heard him utter that particular phrase. "If there are injured people in there, we want to get them out. Get medical assistance for them. You're not going to miss them. Less people inside to keep track of."

There was a moment's silence. Then, "You haven't moved the perimeter back or provided the vehicle I requested. I haven't gotten a thing from you yet, so where's the compromise? Don't call back until you're ready to deal."

The call abruptly disconnected again. The team members took off their headphones and Sharper got up to write notes on the situation board. There was a tap at the back door before it was pulled open. Lewis ducked out to talk to the newcomer. Johnson turned away to summarize the latest conversation to intel over his ear mike radio. A few moments later, Lewis rejoined them. "We've got DMV verification for all the vehicles in the parking lot, and positive ID on the owners. One was reported stolen two days ago from a parking garage on Sixty-first and Locust, a Toyota Camry. That's probably our guy's ride. We've got CSU going over it now."

"Any ID on the hostage down?" Dace asked.

"Walter Hemsworth, security guard for the bank. He's still clothed, so he probably tried to stop the gunman shortly after he entered the bank." Lewis's voice was dispassionate.

Jolie shifted to a more comfortable position and prepared to wait. At the beginning of any armed situation, the hostage taker was running on adrenaline, certain of his power. The longer the ordeal drew out, the more frayed his nerves became. The more hopeless his situation appeared. But it could take hours, or days, for the situation to reach that point.

Something jogged her memory and she looked at Dace. "The HT said 'perimeter.' And again earlier, when he was talking to you. Not move your people back, but 'move the perimeter.'"

"You think law enforcement? Military?"

"Possibly." Grabbing the leather clipboard on the table in front of her with the attached SWAT incident report, she flipped to the legal pad beneath and drew a grid, jotting labels at the top of each column. Writing quickly, she began noting details they'd verified, possibilities and unknowns. There was depressingly little to note, but she wrote down impressions of the gunman from their conversations and the make and model of the stolen Toyota in the first column, and then the words *perimeter—LEO? Military?*—in the second. She'd give Sharper the list to add to the situation board when he was finished with his own notes.

Dace looked on, a thread of amusement sounding in his tone, pitched low enough to reach only her ears. "You and your notes. I don't know how many charts and lists of yours I ran across when I was packing."

Her hand stilled. She kept her attention trained on the legal pad, not trusting herself to look at him. "You moved out of the house?"

"Not much use hanging on to a two-bedroom house for one person." Any trace of humor was absent from his quiet answer. It was as detached as if he were talking to a stranger. Which was exactly what they had become to each other, after… She swallowed. *After.*

His words had been innocuous enough. They shouldn't have had the power to carve a deep furrow of pain through her. Questions rose to her lips, questions that she knew she no longer had a right to ask. And as desperately as she'd like the answers, she couldn't be certain she could deal with that conversation. Especially not here.

She shifted back to the situation at hand. "Who was that on Johnson's radio earlier? Reporting on the visual?"

"Hmm?" He'd withdrawn a pen for the whiteboard and was completing the portions of the SWAT form she hadn't finished. "Oh. Couldn't hear much, but it sounded like Cold Shot. Ava Carter. Lucky for us. She's the best."

A sniper then. These operatives usually had the best vantage points from which to gather intelligence for the incident. But she was surprised that the shooter was female. SWAT was still a male-dominated field, and few women possessed the deadly accuracy with weaponry and the desire to apply that skill to high-stress situations like this.

Herb Johnson rejoined the table. "We've got a positive count on the number inside. The subject is probably the one man who had his face turned away from the camera going in. By the time he got inside, he had a mask pulled down. Besides the ten employees, we have thirteen customers—four men, eight women and a kid. Looks like a boy. Maybe two, two and a half."

The news blindsided Jolie with a force that sent her reeling. Nausea rose, and for one dizzying moment she felt as if she was going to be sick. Her defenses were usually strong enough to protect her against the flood of memory, this paralyzing hurt that was brutal enough to melt her entire system into one oozing pit of pain.

But then there'd be a chance resemblance, a careless word, and the floodgates would open, dragging her back to a past that could still throb like a wound.

"Outside. Now." Dace murmured the order into her ear then got up to head for the doors. Blindly she followed, still stunned.

Once outside he grabbed her arm, pulled her around the corner of the unit so they'd have a semblance of privacy. "I know what you're thinking. Don't."

Helplessly, her gaze met his, lingered.

"We don't know this boy," Dace continued. "We'll do our best for him, and for every other person in that bank. And if you aren't up for that, tell me now."

Another would think his tone cold. Unfeeling. Jolie knew Dace was neither. He was, however, a consummate professional. And so was she. The whiplash of his words helped her remember that.

"I'm okay." But her words sounded weak, even to her own ears. She recognized Dace's logic. Emotion didn't belong in a situation like this. The child was a factor in this case, but the boy was a stranger. An innocent carried into the bank, probably with his mother.

He wasn't Sammy. He wasn't their son.

They'd buried Sammy nearly eighteen months ago.

Chapter 2

Memories flooded Jolie's mind, spilling forth in a mental torrent. The look on Dace's face when the nurse had placed his squalling son in his arms for the first time. Sammy's sweet baby smell after his bath. The staggering joy at seeing his first toothless smile. The all-encompassing anguish of watching his tiny casket lowered into the earth.

Those memories could nearly suffocate her, weight her down under a heavy blanket of sorrow that made a mockery of hope. Long practice had her slamming the door on those images, shoving them aside to focus on the here. The now.

Dace was right. Neither of them knew the child in the bank. But there was no denying the boy's presence there upped the ante dramatically.

She nodded jerkily, started back for the doors.

"Jolie."

Dace's voice, his expression when she flicked a glance at

him, was soft. Her heart stumbled in her chest. She couldn't recall the last time he'd looked at her that way. But it had been well before she'd left him and this city behind. It had been before she'd gone into the nursery one morning to find their son still and cold.

"You sure you're okay?"

"I'm fine." She heard her own oft-repeated phrase on her lips, saw it have the predictable effect on the man beside her. His expression closed and although he didn't move, a part of him shifted away.

And that, too, was familiar.

When they reentered the NOC unit, strategy was being discussed for the next phone call. And when Jolie established contact, she had herself firmly under control again.

"John. How are things going in there? I'm here to help you in any way I can."

"Where's the SUV I requested? How long am I going to have to wait for it?"

There was a new edge to the man's tone. She glanced at Ryder, saw that he'd caught it. The psychologist would help monitor the man's mood to better predict his actions. But before they could do that with any certainty, they needed to learn more about him.

"These things take time," she said easily. "I'm still working on it, though."

"Then we have nothing else to discuss."

From the corner of her eye she saw Dace gesturing but didn't need the reminder to keep the man talking. "Sure we do. Something made you walk into California National Bank this morning. Hard to believe it was just to get the chance to speak to me. You wanted something. Tell me about that."

"That's easy," came the disembodied answer. "This is where they keep the money."

She heard voices coming from Johnson's headset, and the man moved away from the table so the gunman wouldn't overhear. "So that's what this is about? The money? Why'd you choose this bank?"

"It was here. I was here. Seemed like fate. Do you believe in fate, Jolie?"

"I believe in personal responsibility. In doing the right thing. It's not too late for you to do the right thing, John. Things haven't gone so wrong yet that you can't walk away from this. I want to help you with that." She didn't mention the dead security guard. If they were to convince the gunman to surrender, they had to make him believe he had a chance if he did things their way. "Why don't you come out before things get out of hand?"

There was a soft laugh on the other side of the line. "You're good. I can see why Recker let you take over. But unfortunately for you, you're not dealing with an idiot. Thanks for the offer, but I like my chances better if we follow my plan."

She glanced at Dace, who was reading a note Johnson had written and given to him. "What plan is that?"

"You get the perimeter pulled back. Bring the car up to the back doors. I leave quietly with the cash and, of course, a couple hostages to ensure my safety. We all live happily ever after."

As fairy tales went, his was particularly far-fetched. There was no way his demands would be met. Before he would be allowed to leave the vicinity, an assault-and-rescue operation would be staged. Such an operation drastically increased the odds of injury to those inside. But she was charged with the task of making sure it never came to that.

"We're working on that for you, John. We want a happy ending as much as you do. But these things take time. You know what bureaucracy is like, right? And while we're waiting, you've got things to take care of, too. The people inside are going to need to use the restroom soon. Maybe food. Water. We can assist you with that."

"I don't give a damn what they need." The earlier control the gunman had displayed was definitely thinning. "They aren't my concern."

"Couple dozen people who can't use the bathroom can be cause for anyone's concern," she returned, injecting a note of amusement into her voice that she was far from feeling. "Especially if they're all being kept in a small area. Where are they, in the vault? Pretty soon the money's not going to smell so good."

There was silence on the other end, leaving Jolie with no idea what the other man was thinking. "If there's anyone in there who's injured, John, now's the time to send them out. Wounded people are just another headache for you."

Dace touched her arm, handed her the note to read.

"On the contrary, Jolie. Wounded people will soon become *your* headache. Because if my demands aren't met by the next time we talk, I'm going to start shooting people in here."

That got her attention. "You don't want to do that, John." Her tone was firm. "I can help you out of this thing. I swear it. But if you harm anyone else in there, your options narrow drastically. You're smart enough to realize that. I know you are."

A click was her only answer.

Slowly, she lowered the phone while Dace crumpled the note in his hand. "So there's a visual of him in the lobby?" That much, at least, she'd been able to read before the HT had reclaimed her focus.

He nodded. "He's still wearing the mask, which is good news."

Maintaining his disguise meant he still thought there was

a way out of this, so he was taking pains not to be identified. It was when his hopes of walking away alive were dashed that they had reason to worry.

But there was something in the way Dace was regarding her that had trepidation stirring in her belly. "What else?" Whatever it was, there was no doubt he'd give it to her straight. Dace had always been honest to a fault.

I don't know if I love you. How could I? It's too soon, for either of us. But I know I'll love this baby, if you'll go through with the pregnancy. I'll do right by it. By both of you. Give me a chance, Jolie. Give us a chance.

His earnest honesty had disarmed defenses that she'd once thought stronger. Had undermined common sense and shredded reason. In retrospect she still couldn't understand how he'd circumvented a lifetime of caution and compelled her to reach for something she'd never before dared hope for.

"What else?" she repeated, in an effort to shake those memories from her head.

"He had the boy on his shoulders. One hand around both the child's wrists, to pull him down to drape over his head."

A chill broke out over Jolie's arms. She rubbed them absently, muttering, "Smart bastard." And totally cold, totally unfeeling, to use a child like that. In situations like this, if snipers were used to neutralize a gunman, they went for a head shot to produce instant incapacitation. There was no doubt the HT knew that. He'd positioned the child to protect his brain stem.

"Sounding more and more like someone well versed in law enforcement tactics," Dace noted grimly.

"Or someone who's done his homework," Dr. Ryder put in. "He's covered every base."

Skepticism was written on Sharper's square face. "Hard to believe an LEO would think he could get away with bank robbery."

"But he has been getting away with it," Lewis said grimly. "Twelve banks have been hit in a tristate area in the past three months. All have been smaller branches like this one. He's in and out in under ten minutes. Rough estimates have the take so far at over thirty million."

Jolie whistled under her breath. Smaller banks would have less cash on hand than their larger counterparts, but they'd also be easier to case. Fewer employees. Lower risk for complications.

Then the full ramification of Lewis's words struck her. Bank robbery was a federal offense, and if this was one of a series, there was an ongoing investigation. In an undertone, she said to Dace, "How long do you guess we have before the feds step in?"

"I'm sort of surprised they haven't shown up yet."

His voice, his expression, was sardonic. He'd never been the Bureau's biggest fan.

"Have there been any victims in the prior robberies?"

"Three." Lewis worked a knot out of his shoulder. "So this guy isn't afraid to leave bodies behind."

Which was very bad news for them. And even worse for the hostages inside.

The CCL ducked out of the NOC unit to head over to the command center. While he was gone the team added details on the situation board. Using the floor plans of the bank, Johnson showed Sharper the positions of the SWAT personnel. All the known details were drawn in, down to the location of the throw phone. They used sticky notes to add unknowns, like the position of the hostages.

Jolie handed over her list and Sharper started a similar grid on the board.

Lewis returned as they were finishing. Something in his expression alerted Jolie. "We're arranging to bring in a station wagon to park out front. You know what to do."

Dace and Jolie exchanged a glance. "What's the rush?" he asked.

The CCL sat down heavily. "Don't worry. Mendel is committed to the negotiation process. But the HT has issued two verbal threats and he's placing a child in danger. We have to be ready to act fast."

Usually a vehicle was provided only when a tactical resolution was being planned. It caused the HT to leave his surroundings and enter the SWAT team's controlled environment.

And under any other circumstances, Jolie would be objecting vehemently about rushing the process. But the boy inside being used as a human shield changed things. She still hoped for a peaceful resolution. But she wasn't going to quibble about being prepared for the alternative.

Of course the HT wasn't going to be allowed to dictate the terms. There was no way the SUV he'd requested would be brought in. The vehicles were too hard to see into. Had too much interior space. Most likely the station wagon was an older model, and it would be totally messed with. Although the gas tank would show full, it would have very little fuel. The radio would be on full blast, along with the heater, to serve as distractions in case the gunman ever made it to the car.

The likelihood of him getting that far was slim, but every contingency would be planned for.

Next time they established contact with the gunman, they'd work a trade. And since it didn't seem as though there were any injured inside needing medical assistance, she knew exactly what her priority would be.

"Let's see if he'll exchange the boy."

After a brief hesitation, Dace said quietly, "Of course. But you know he won't, Jolie. Are you prepared for that?"

She was. Of course she was. The man had found a crudely effective way of ensuring his own survival. It didn't matter how good the snipers were, there was no way a "weapons loose" command was going to be given with a child blocking a clear head shot. And that was the only guaranteed way to make sure the HT didn't fire a recoil shot before dropping.

"Chances are he's carrying a cell. Any number of the hostages probably have them, too. But he didn't insist I direct further communications to a cell phone, which he could use out of sight, away from the skylights."

Dace nodded. "He wants us to know what the stakes are. Wants us to see the risk of injury to the boy. This guy has anticipated worst-case scenarios. We already know he's familiarized himself with LEO procedure. He may be aware that we have the technology to disable the cells once we arrive on the scene."

Jolie settled back on her chair, determination and dread mingling. Simultaneous realizations occurred. There were going to be far more dangerous complications to this situation than the relationship between her and Dace.

And however it ended, it wasn't going to be easy.

"You've got your vehicle, John." Dace was still wondering why the HT had asked for him. Jolie had handled the process of lowering the gunman's expectations from an SUV and talking him through law enforcement's approach with the vehicle. It had turned into a long, drawn-out procedure. "Keys are in it."

"Is this your doing, Recker? Pretty far cry from the SUV I asked for, isn't it?"

"We're doing the best we can for you here, John. We wanted something with a police radio in it so we could still communicate with you."

There was a short, harsh laugh. "You probably got the crate right off the police impound lot. Turn it on and leave it running for a few minutes. I want proof it's in working order. And you still haven't pulled the perimeter back. Looks like more cops out there than ever."

"One step at a time. We gave you something you want. Now it's time for you to reciprocate."

"I'm not in a giving mood, Recker." Over four hours had passed since the alarm inside had been pressed. Their intelligence officers had kept track of the movement inside the bank, which had been minimal. Aside from the guard's body, only the HT and the boy had been seen, and then only when the HT had answered the phone. The other hostages had not been sighted.

Jolie's conversations with John, however, had also served as a diversion. Tactical had taken the opportunity to affix a listening device to a window at the corner of the building. Now they could hear what was going on inside. At the moment, however, there seemed little to report.

The crowd outside had grown. As soon as the media had gotten wind of what was going down at California National, journalists and TV anchors had descended on the vicinity like a swarm of locusts. The extra LEO personnel had been necessary for crowd control. An information center had been set up, since it was far easier to release controlled information to the media than to risk them trying to sneak closer for an exclusive. No doubt among the ongoing live reporting the talking heads were interspersing commentary from their versions of "experts" of various occupations, giving self-important assessments of the gunman. The hostages. And suggesting endless scenarios for a fascinated public.

Dace wondered if "John" had access to a television inside. Some hostage takers reveled in the notoriety, their one brush

with fame. But he didn't think the gunman inside was motivated by anything other than what he'd first revealed: money.

"You have to be thirsty. Hungry. We can deliver food.
Whatever you want. Easier to think on a full stomach, I
always find."

No answer. But the other man was still there. He could hear
him breathing on the other end of the line. Keeping his voice
easy, Dace continued. "What's your favorite? Ham sand-
wiches? Pizza? We can get enough for you to feed everyone
inside. But we need to talk about the boy, John. Tyler Mills.
He's only twenty-two months old. Kid that age needs diapers.
Regular meals. Naps. He has to be getting cranky. Now's the
time to send him out. Believe me, you don't want to be
dealing with a two-year-old who's short on sleep."

"The kid stays." John's voice, when he finally spoke, was
flat. Emotionless. "But you can send in the food. Diapers.
And something for him to drink."

"Good idea. I'll get on that right away. But I want you to
think more about the boy. Tyler. You don't need him. How
about an exchange, the boy for the vehicle."

"Like I said, I'm keeping the kid." There was a hesitation.
"But I'm a fair man. I'll give you two different hostages. One
now, and another when the food arrives."

Dace saw Jolie gesturing in vehement disapproval, but he
answered, "Fair enough. But it'd be best to send the boy out,
John. All those people inside, you don't need him."

There was an eerie laugh. "I *do* need him. He's my good-
luck charm. Keeps your snipers from getting trigger-happy,
doesn't he?"

"We all want a peaceful ending to this. We're not looking
for anyone to get hurt. You need to start thinking about how
we can get everyone home safe. You included. That's what's
important here."

"Now there's where you're wrong, Recker." There was chilly amusement in the other man's voice. "What's important is me walking out of here with the cash. The rest is your agenda, not mine."

"Hey, we're on the same page, John." Dace didn't let a hint of frustration tinge his words. "I don't want anything happening to you. We're ready to do what it takes so everyone gets what they want."

A click was his only answer. Dace set the phone down, raising his brows at the group. Dr. Ryder said, looking thoughtful, "I think we were dead-on with our first impression of this guy. Likes to be in control. May even be used to a position of authority. He uses a totally different tone with you, Dace, than he does with Jolie. I still think he believes she's a soft touch because she's a woman." He glanced at Jolie. "No offense. But when things don't go the way he wants, he demands to talk to the male. It's a man he expects will be making the decisions. You also get the blame when he doesn't like how things work out."

It was very possible. But an entirely different thought had been forming in Dace's mind during the course of the last conversation. He leaned over to look at the notes Jolie had been making. He was struck at once by the similarity of their thinking. When it came to their work, at least, he and Jolie disagreed on very little. It had been their private life that had ended with neither able to communicate with the other.

Which was ironic as hell, given their background as trained negotiators. Why did it seem so much simpler for him to talk to a sociopath like the one locked inside that bank than to the woman he'd lived with? Had a child with?

He had a mental flash of the two of them standing at the edge of Sammy's grave. Such a small hole for an equally tiny casket. Jolie had been standing beside him, but they hadn't been touching. It had been as if each of them had a force field surrounding them, keeping everyone else at a distance. Family. Friends. Each other. It had been all he could do to cope with the pain gnawing a hole through his chest without howling his rage, his desolation to the world. He'd sleep-walked through the entire process. Planning the service. The funeral. Greeting the mourners. Responding to the flowers and donations that had been sent. It hadn't been until a week afterward that the numbness had worn off, leaving only the bone-crushing grief behind.

He hadn't reached for Jolie then either.

"Okay, I'm going out on a limb here." Jolie interrupted his thoughts. "But his mention of the snipers got me thinking. We know he did his homework on the potential police response. But even given his suspicion that snipers are waiting, he walks freely across the open lobby to answer the phone each time. Yeah, he's using the child for protection. But he's still exposing himself to a body-mass shot that could be a back-up target as long as his head is unexposed."

The same thing had occurred to Dace during the last con-versation. "He's wearing Kevlar. Or hell, maybe he's even got himself a Tac-Vest. Feels confident. Sure, it leaves his legs exposed, but the worst that could happen is getting his knee blown away. Even then, there's plenty of time to kill the boy."

He looked at Johnson. "The security video…what was the suspected gunman wearing?"

"Jeans, sneakers, long baggy UCLA sweatshirt and a matching cap pulled down low," came the response. "Wearing a backpack. Must have had the gun concealed inside it."

"Smart prick," Lewis muttered. "Went in prepared. What's everyone's take? Are we wearing him down at all?"

The team members were silent for a moment. "He's

tiring," Jolie said finally. "And the exchange is an important concession."

"He's playing ball," Dace agreed. "But I'm not ready to claim we're anywhere near breaking him down yet."

Dr. Ryder agreed. "He still feels in control. The decision to release the hostages was his, made on his terms. I don't think he's an imminent threat. But he does still believe he's walking out of there with the cash."

Lewis nodded. "I'll let command center know about the hostage release." He slipped out of the back door of the vehicle.

Herb Johnson had his head down, listening to a voice on his mike. "He's disappeared down the hallway again," he reported.

"There's only the vice-president's office and the vault down that way," Sharper interjected. "Our guess about keeping the hostages in the vault must be right."

Johnson bent his head, listening to his earpiece intently. "He's marching a man toward the door. Has the kid draped over his shoulders still. The boy is crying."

Dace shot a glance at Jolie, but she wasn't looking at him. Studying her profile, however, he could see that the muscles in her jaw were tight. The involvement of the boy was hard on her. Odd how he could read her emotions better now than he'd been able to eighteen months earlier. She'd shut down then. They both had. And when he'd lashed out at her for her seeming lack of feeling, he'd been lashing out as much at himself. At fate. At a cruel God that had snatched away his greatest joy.

Just the memory of the accusation he'd leveled sent a burn of shame through him. Unable to reach her emotionally, he'd reacted with anger. Anger was about the only feeling that hadn't hurt back then.

But it had hurt her. Them. Because a few short weeks after

Sammy's funeral, she'd left. And then there'd been no reaching her at all.

"The first hostage is out," Johnson reported. He listened a few more seconds before continuing, "It's a man. Naked. And inside the HT's allowing one man and one woman to use the restrooms while he watches. He doesn't leave himself exposed."

The hostage would be given a blanket and led to the command center for debriefing. He could have valuable information about the gunman inside. And they had to be certain the released man was indeed a hostage, and not the HT himself, mounting a bold escape.

"He's showing concern for the hostages," Dr. Ryder said with a degree of relief. "Holding them in the vault kept them separate from the HT. Made it easier for him to avoid seeing them as human. This may be a very good sign."

"Might be a good time to distract him with a call," Sharper suggested.

"Go ahead and try," Dace told Jolie. But he knew the HT wasn't going to answer right now. The man was too smart for that.

But then, maybe he was giving this guy too much credit. How smart could he really be if he still thought there was any way he was going to be allowed to walk away from this thing?

Twenty minutes crawled by, with Johnson relaying the intel about the activity inside. The HT had worked his way through most of the captives before a rap sounded at the double back doors.

They were pulled open, revealing Lewis's grim demeanor. Behind him Dace could see several unfamiliar faces, and his stomach took a nosedive. The effing-B-I had arrived.

"Officers." The dispassionate tone was belied by the fury glittering in the man's eyes. "The feds have decided to crash the party. They'll be taking over negotiations."

Chapter 3

It was more than a little anticlimactic to be relegated to onlooker after taking an active role in neutralizing the situation. Dace stood a few feet away from Jolie, near the edge of the inner perimeter, chafing at the change. An hour had ticked by since they'd briefed the feds and left the NOC unit. If they hadn't been ordered by Lewis to stand by, he'd have gone back to the precinct to duty. At least there he'd be allowed to do something productive. There was no way the feds were going to accept help from the locals.

"Hey, Jolie!"

Dace turned his head to see Ron Wetzel, a sergeant from Jolie's old precinct, pause as he was hurrying by.

"I didn't know you were back in these parts. Had enough of busting movie stars and director wannabes and came back to the real people, huh?"

"You guessed it, Ron." There was none of the guardedness

in her tone that was present when she spoke to Dace. Her voice was friendly. "The glamour got to be too much for me. Give me a barricade any day over taking burglary complaints from self-important wine growers."

"Where were you assigned there?"

Dace listened unabashedly to their conversation, more interested in her answers than he wanted to admit.

"Fifth precinct. Partnered with Selma Garcia. You know her?"

"I don't think so." Someone nearby shouted the man's name, and he started to move away. "Hey, come on down to the Blue Lagoon sometime. See some of the guys."

"I'll do that. Tell everyone hello for me."

"You got it."

Dace kept his gaze trained on the bank, what he could see of it from this distance. So the rumor he'd heard had been right. She'd gone from here to the LAPD. He'd asked around after she'd moved out. After he found she'd changed her cellphone number and left her job. Officers in her old precinct had been pretty closemouthed, but he'd heard she might have headed to LA. And that had been the end of it. Hard to find someone in a city of four million who obviously hadn't wanted to be found. At least not by him.

That's when the bitterness had swamped him and he'd forced himself to stop thinking about her for good.

At least he'd given it a damn good try.

But those efforts were going to be shot to hell if he had to see her every time they were called out to an incident. Metro City PD was large enough for them to coexist without running into each other often. With a population of half a million and a police force of over eight hundred, she could have been back in the city a year without them ever bumping into each other.

But instead, they'd been thrown together on the same HNT

unit, requiring them to work closely together on volatile incidents. Which only went to prove yet again that fate was a fickle bitch with a mean sense of humor.

"What happened to Rob Marlow?"

Her question interrupted his dark thoughts. He and Marlow had been paired on HNT for three years, and the man had been his mentor in incident response.

"Took his twenty and out last month. He and his wife are moving to Burbank. And Thompson took a promotion and left HNT in January."

"Burbank?" Her voice sounded as incredulous as he'd felt when his partner had relayed the news. "What are they—"

"So are you going to ask to be reassigned, or am I?" He didn't glance in her direction, but knew she'd heard him. Sensed the stillness that came over her. "This is a distraction. For both of us. We can't afford distractions in situations like this."

"I don't know. I thought we did all right together in there."

He did look at her then, anger flaring abruptly at her even tone. Was she saying their proximity didn't bother her at all? That it didn't elicit the unwelcome bits of memory? The welter of suppressed emotion? He studied her, noting her composed expression, which gave away nothing of her thoughts. That had always been the problem—he'd never known what the hell she was thinking. Feeling. And rarely had she told him, even when he'd asked.

He'd had sex with her. Lived with her. Had a child with her. But he'd never really known her.

"I'll ask for the transfer then," he said flatly. Their messy personal history wasn't something that could be swept neatly under the rug. And it would be unprofessional to enter situations like these and pretend otherwise. There was just too much at stake.

"No." Although her expression didn't change, her voice

sounded strained. "It wouldn't be fair for you to go. This is your squad. Your friends. If I'd known you'd returned to Alpha Squad I'd never have accepted this assignment. I'll ask for a reassignment."

He nodded curtly and returned his attention to the bank front. The food had been delivered, but it still sat untouched in front of the bank door. The second hostage hadn't been released yet. What the heck was going on with the negotiations?

No answers were forthcoming. Reluctantly, he slanted a glance at Jolie. "What will you tell them?"

"I don't know yet. I don't want to hurt my chances of being reassigned, and there's only one other HNT unit anyway. I'll have to see if that team has a vacancy."

Dace went silent, refusing to feel guilty. She was bilingual, which made her a good prospect for any HNT vacancy that came up. And it wasn't his problem if she couldn't get a different position. Hell, if she'd been assigned to the other squad, they wouldn't be doing this now. He could have gone along for months, never even knowing she was around. Whoever had said ignorance was bliss had been dead-on.

"I'll think of something."

"You could always leave again. You're good at that."

The instant the words left his mouth he wanted to retract them. He didn't often stoop to being petty and mean. But right now he was feeling petty and he was feeling mean. When she didn't respond he reached out, snagged the sunglasses off the bridge of her nose and watched her eyes. Sometimes he could read there what he couldn't see in her expression.

They stared at each other in silence and for an instant their surroundings faded away. For the second time that day he felt like he'd been sucker punched. Her eyes were laser blue, an unbelievably pure color. Sammy had had his mother's eyes with Dace's dark hair.

But he'd never seen Sammy's eyes filled with the misery he read in hers.

"Jolie…"

"Recker! Conrad! Get back to the NOC unit!"

Lewis's barked order shattered the moment, and Jolie retrieved the glasses he'd removed before heading back toward the converted ambulance. Dace followed, strangely shaken. He had no idea what he'd been about to say earlier, but whatever it might have been would have been a mistake. It was too late for words between them. There was too much history, most of it painful. Better that they get through the next few hours and then go their separate ways.

He'd spent the past sixteen months getting some sort of order back into his life. New apartment. New furniture. New women. He'd moved on, and he had no desire to revisit whatever had existed between him and Jolie Conrad.

There was a cluster of individuals standing outside the NOC unit, too many to fit inside. The tension, when they joined the group, was palpable. Besides Lewis, Dace and herself, there were nine others, five of whom Jolie recognized as the agents who had taken over the negotiation.

"Special Agents Dawson, Hart and Truman." Lewis gestured to each newcomer in turn, before indicating the lone female. "And Special Agent in Charge Fenholt, all out of the Los Angeles field office. The FBI's negotiators haven't had much luck with the HT since our team left."

"I'm sure given enough time, the gunman would respond to the Bureau's negotiators," Hart said stiffly. Jolie wondered if he was as young as he looked. He could have been a pledge for a college fraternity.

"We don't have time," Lewis said bluntly. "We just wasted an hour."

"That's right." SAC Fenholt was a woman who looked to be pushing the Bureau's mandatory retirement age. Her dark hair, liberally streaked with gray, was pulled severely back from a face with strong bones and an angular jaw. "Looking over a summary of your contacts, I didn't think we had anything to lose by trying a new team. But the HT hasn't answered a call since he discovered the change in negotiators. He demands to speak to Conrad." Fenholt flicked a glance her way. "Each time he answers and doesn't hear your voice he hangs up again. It doesn't make sense to waste more time trying to reestablish a rapport with different negotiators. We want you two to resume the duty, under our supervision."

Dace sent a pointed look at the crowd of individuals. "Sure. Maybe we can stack agents in a corner of the NOC so we don't have to sit on each other's laps."

Fenholt ignored his sardonic tone. "In addition to you two, we'll keep Agents Meadow and Spading on the team to serve as scribe and profiler." She indicated two of the men from the FBI negotiation unit that had replaced the MCPD squad. "Special Agent Dawson will act as command center liaison. Special Agent Truman will serve as tactical liaison." Truman, a forty-ish man with a graying buzz cut and a permanent scowl, pulled open the NOC door and heaved himself inside. Jolie and Dace stepped aside, waiting for all the other agents to enter first.

Fenholt paused, shot them a hard look. "Get the subject talking again. I understand that threats were issued earlier. I want him defused."

"Why don't you let us first assess the changes to his mood since you reassigned negotiators?" Jolie kept her voice bland but she saw the flicker in the woman's expression before she turned and walked away. She hadn't made a new friend, but she couldn't bring herself to care.

Jolie and Dace sat down at the table inside. She scanned the notes that had been added to the situation board in their absence. Other than the HT's demands for their return, there was no new information except for a few tactical details.

Dace picked up the phone and handed it to her. "He's asking for you, so go ahead and make the call. We may have to make up some ground with him after this."

She nodded, scanning the other members as each picked up headphones. Special Agent Dawson sat closest to the door. He hadn't said a word through the entire exchange. His face, the color of fresh-brewed coffee, was completely expressionless. Yet she couldn't shake the feeling that every word she and Dace uttered from here on out would be weighed and evaluated.

She made the call, let it ring. Eight times. Nine. Then it was picked up, but no one spoke.

"John, it's Jolie Conrad. How are you? Everything okay in there?"

"Where's Recker?"

"He's here. Do you want to talk to him?"

"That's okay." The strain in his voice eased infinitesimally. "Took them long enough to get you two back. They were feds, right? The other two bozos on the line earlier? What'd they do, come in and claim jurisdiction?"

Although the words brought a smile to her lips, Jolie said only, "We all want the same thing here, John. For you to get through this okay. For the people inside to remain unharmed. Everybody still all right in there? I see the food has been delivered. It's still setting outside the door. You've got to be getting hungry."

"I'll send someone out for it."

"And then it will be time to release the second hostage. That was our earlier agreement." She glanced at Dace, who gave her a slight nod. "I know you want to do the right thing."

"We never agreed that you'd turn this over to the feds, though, did we? I feel a little betrayed, Jolie." Despite his words, the man sounded calm. "You don't want to do that again."

"It was just bureaucratic politics. You understand that, right?"

"Now you understand why I went into business for myself." There was dark humor in the words. "Being your own boss can be very rewarding."

She didn't need Dace's gesture to pursue this line. Anything they could find out about the captor's background would assist them in judging whom they were dealing with. And what he was capable of. "You sound like you have some experience with difficult bosses."

"Enough to know that I never want another one. Nine-to-five wasn't my thing."

"I hear you there. The routine can get tiresome. What about it—"

There was a loud clatter, then the line went dead.

"What the hell happened?" Jolie threw out the question even as she tried to ring the phone again. "Find out what's going on."

Truman exchanged his earphones for a radio headset and listened intently. "The kid is putting up a struggle. Sounds like the HT is having trouble subduing him." He turned away to speak urgently into the mike, alerting tactical that a hostage was about to be released. Special Agent Dawson slipped away, presumably to the command center.

Jolie tried the phone several times, but got no answer. Agent Meadow added notes from the last conversation to the situation board. Spading looked at her, his pale blue gaze assessing. "Sounds like he missed you."

"We were making headway when our team got pulled," she said shortly. "We'd won concessions. But another hour's been wasted and the child has to be exhausted." The HT didn't strike Jolie as the patient sort. "The longer this goes on, the more upset he's going to get."

"An increasing danger to the child will be a big consideration in the decision for a tactical response," Spading pointed out.

"As it should be," she retorted. There was a tense knot in her chest that wouldn't dissipate until Truman delivered the tactical report about what was happening in the bank. She threw an impatient look at the man, but his expression as he listened to his headset gave away nothing. "But I don't think the HT's at that point yet. He still thinks he's going to get out of this thing."

Spading gave a slow nod. "Agreed. But sooner or later it's going to occur to him just how unlikely that is, and that's when he's at his most dangerous."

"Unless we convince him to give up by that point," Dace interjected.

Finally, Truman took off the headset. "A second hostage has been released unharmed. Hopefully he'll be able to provide more intelligence than the first one did."

Dawson picked that moment to reenter the NOC unit. "Special Agent in Charge Fenholt is growing increasingly concerned about the child's welfare. She's putting a time limit on negotiations. You've got no more than two hours before we mount an assault."

"So far none of the hostages have been harmed." The snap in Dace's voice was barely discernible, but it was there. "An assault ensures injuries. Time limits are counterproductive when talking to—"

"Two hours," the man repeated, taking his seat again.

"Go ahead and make contact," Dace instructed.

But Jolie already had the phone ringing. And although

she'd half expected otherwise, John answered after only a moment. "You okay in there, John?" First and foremost, a negotiator had to express concern for the hostage taker. It was crucial to maintain the rapport that was built one painstaking conversation at a time. A rapport the feds had disrupted with their arrival.

"I'm fine. You've got your second person released. I've kept my word."

"Never had any doubt about that." There was definite tension showing in his voice, Jolie decided. "But I'd be even more excited to see you come out. Unharmed. How about it? Put down your weapon and come out with your hands raised. That's the surest way to end this thing peacefully. I don't want to see you get hurt."

"I'll be out. When the time is right. I want the car's gas tank full. See to that."

Jolie sent a questioning look at Dawson, who shrugged. "I'll check on that for you, John."

"I don't want anyone charging in here," he warned. "I'll come out, but I set the timeline."

"That's good. I like to hear you talking about coming out. No one wants to go in there, John. No one wants to hurt you."

"Don't kid yourself." The HT gave a short laugh. "Everyone wants something in this life. And there's not much doubt what all the cops out there are waiting for."

"What do you think they're waiting for?"

"Me. Getting carried away in a body bag."

Jolie leaned forward, elbows propped on the table. "John, you're wrong about that." Her voice was firm. "The best sight we could get is you walking out of there on your own volition, bringing this thing to a peaceful end. Seeing all those people in there unharmed. That's what we want. Doesn't sound so bad, does it?"

"You do this a lot?"

She followed his sudden switch of topic seamlessly. "You mean talk to people in trouble? I've had some experience. Lots of people just want to be listened to. I'm here to listen, John."

Dace slid a slip of paper into her view. At least he'd taken the care to print, always a bonus when it came to reading his handwriting. She read the directive and glanced his way, giving him a short nod.

"No one really listens," the man on the other end of the phone said flatly. "It's everyone for himself in this world. Yeah, you have friends, coworkers, if you're punching a clock. But in the end, you're alone. And people who don't recognize that are suckers."

The words struck a chord. There was a time when the sentiment was not so far from Jolie's own attitude. People invariably let you down. It was one of life's absolutes. It was infinitely easier, wiser, to rely on yourself. But that was before she met Dace. Before she'd had Sammy. Before she'd been the one to let the people in her life down. Big time.

"You forgot family," she said smoothly, bringing up the topic on Dace's note. "You have family, John?"

There was a pause, and the ensuing silence was charged with emotion. In the background Jolie could hear Tyler fussing. Calling for his mother. She blocked out the sound. Blocked out everything but the man's answer.

"Yeah, you're right. Family matters. About the only thing that does, when it gets down to it. How about you? You have any family?"

And suddenly the charged emotion had nothing to do with the man's response. Now the air of expectation emanated from Dace.

Jolie hesitated. "No," she said finally, taking care not to

look in Dace's direction. "There's just me. But if there's someone we can call for you, John, you need to let me know. We can make that happen."

"No, I'll be talking to him soon enough. When I walk out of here."

"When will that be, John? When are you planning on walking out of there?"

"Soon. I'll let you know." And with that the line went dead.

Disconnecting, Jolie looked at Dace. "So what do you think? Is he considering giving up, or does he still think he's taking that vehicle and heading out to Never-Never-Land?"

"He's hanging on to the thought of escape." Spading nodded agreement while Dawson said nothing. "We still have a ways to go in convincing him to give up." Dace scratched his jaw, which was already showing signs of a shadow. He'd often shaved twice a day while they were together. The memory snuck into her subconscious, unbidden. Before he'd join her in bed, his jaw would be smooth, inviting her fingers. Her lips. Whatever else had gone on between them, they'd never lacked communication in bed.

A slow heat suffused her body and Jolie forced her gaze away. It was only when actual words were needed that they both had fallen short.

"The way he's still talking about that car, I don't think he's given up on the idea of getting out of there with a few hostages."

"Maybe not." With effort she shifted her thoughts firmly back into the present. "But we have time, if we can convince Fenholt to drop this ridiculous time limit and allow us to continue the process."

"Activity inside." They all stared at Truman as he re-counted the information coming through on his headset.

"He's bringing people to the lobby by twos. Handing them zip cords and having them bind one another's hands and feet." He sent a meaningful look to Dawson. "He's lining them up on the floor below the windows."

Without a word, Agent Dawson left the NOC. "He's protecting himself against a tactical assault," Jolie said.

Spading added, "His actions aren't that of a man getting ready to give up."

"His actions also aren't escalating," Dace countered. "He hasn't been violent. Hasn't made threats for a couple hours. We've got no reason to rush this."

But they were being rushed. Fenholt's time limit hung over their heads, the minutes ticking away. Jolie glanced at her watch and reached for the phone. They couldn't make progress when they weren't engaged in negotiations.

Dawson returned just then. His face, usually so impassive, was set in hard grim lines. "Establishing contact again? Good. Tell him the vehicle is going to be gassed and running, pulled up closer to the back door."

"What?" Dace exchanged a look with Jolie. "Why? What's the rush? We've got over an hour left on Fenholt's timeline. The HT is still talking. There's no reason to deliberately draw him out now."

"You know the procedure. Just work the subject."

Jolie felt the frustration coming off Dace in waves, but concentrated only on the ringing phone. Communication between command and HNT unit was a sensitive process at the best of times. As negotiators they had to know enough about what was going on to sound knowledgeable to the gunman. But it was dangerous for them to be apprised of tactical plans. There was too much risk that they'd say something to alert the hostage taker.

That was hard enough to accept when she trusted the

people in command. That wasn't the case here. Foreboding knotted her chest.

"Jolie." The HT's familiar voice sounded.

"John. How are things going in there? Have you given any more thought to my earlier suggestion?"

"About coming out? I've done nothing but think about getting out of here since this morning, so yeah, I guess you can say I've been thinking about it. Been taking precautions in here, too. Just in case some of those cops get anxious to get inside."

"You don't have to worry about that."

"It's good to hear, and it's not that I don't trust you, Jolie. Really." His tone was sardonic. "Let's just call my measures a little extra insurance."

"Tell me about what you're doing, John."

"Nothing more than a little rearranging. No one's been hurt. But the hostages are now tied up and lying under the windows and across the doorways. Do you know what that means, Jolie?"

She did. The measure guaranteed that a SWAT entry would injure hostages. "That's unnecessary. I've already said no one's coming in to get you. Why would we? You're coming out. You told me so yourself."

"And I'm a man of my word. Proved that earlier, didn't I? By sending those hostages out."

"You did. It was the right thing to do, John. And I've got some good news for you. Your vehicle is going to be pulled up closer to the back door of the bank. Can you see it?"

"Somehow I thought the feds would start seeing things my way." Dark humor tinged his tone. "I'll almost be sorry to say goodbye, Jolie."

And with that, the line abruptly went dead.

With studied control, she set the phone down carefully on

the table. Jaw tight, she speared a look at Dawson, who was watching her. "Fenholt's hurrying this."

"It's her call to make."

Shaking her head vehemently, Jolie retorted, "She's crazy. She wants to take him down as he tries for the vehicle? There's no way to avoid injuring a hostage. How's that going to play on the national news this evening?"

"Better than twenty-three dead hostages would, I expect. Our guys are good. They'll minimize the casualties."

She gripped the edge of the table tightly and fought for control. "One of those casualties is almost certainly going to be a two-year-old boy. She has to consider the fallout if she—"

"Ms. Conrad." The finality of Dawson's tone stopped her. "The decision has already been made. The HT is probably heading out the door as we speak."

Dace put a hand on her shoulder, but Jolie shrugged it off and made her way out the back to round the vehicle and stare toward the bank. The building blocked her view of whatever was transpiring outside its back doors. Helplessness flooded through her. Her part here was likely done. For good or bad, the outcome was fast approaching and there wasn't a thing more she could do about it.

It was useless to replay her conversations with the HT in her mind, questioning whether she could have done anything differently. The subject had set this whole thing in motion once he'd walked into that bank. The one thing she was sure of was that somehow Tyler was part of this final act, as well.

The first explosion rocked the ground beneath her and had her slapping a hand to the NOC unit for support. The second and third battered her eardrums, coupled with the sound of shattering glass from the bank. A trio of fireballs rose like blazing rockets toward the dusky sky.

Chapter 4

"We believe at least three remote-activated explosive devices were placed in the area behind the bank. Possibly housed in magnetic boxes attached to the light poles here, here and here." Special Agent in Charge Fenholt indicated the spots on a hand-drawn map hanging on the whiteboard, showing the back of the building. "They could have been placed there when the HT was scouting the location or even as early as this morning before he headed inside. A driver in an armored car used the distraction caused by the detonations to crash through barricades here—" she pointed at the corner on the street in back of the bank "—traveling at a high rate of speed. One local officer was hit and injured by the vehicle. Three others, including one of our agents, were killed in the blasts."

There was a grim silence in the conference room following this piece of news. Dace stretched his legs out under the table, taking care not to brush Jolie seated beside him. The debriefing promised to last well into the night, and like the past several hours of the incident, the feds were running the show. He doubted he was the only one in the room braced for the inevitable blame game to ensue.

Extra tables and chairs had to be brought in to accommodate all the personnel in the room. The local SWAT/HNT unit was accounted for, as well as the FBI's SWAT squad and Fenholt's team.

"What's the total casualty and injury count?" Metro City Police Chief Carl Sanders sat at the conference table flanked by his deputy chief, Robert Grey. The chief had an aging football player's still-solid physique, fading gingery hair and a shrewd blue gaze that stripped through all defenses.

Fenholt walked back to her chair and consulted some notes bundled together on the table before her. "Forty-seven were taken to local hospitals for treatment, including the hostages inside the bank. They all suffered various lacerations from the flying glass when the windows blew out. Suffice to say, as a distraction, the explosives served admirably. Under the circumstances, the casualties were contained."

Dace gave an incredulous snort. Picking up a remote, Fenholt turned on a large TV mounted in one corner of the room. "We've obtained this footage from KCHM, shot from their helicopter." Silently, they all watched the HT exit the back door of the bank, with Tyler Mills on his shoulders. He wore a red backpack and was carrying bank bags. All eyes and weapons would have been on the man as he headed to the station wagon. With hindsight it was easy to see the subject duck at the last moment, seeking shelter behind the vehicle's bumper just seconds before the explosions and the resulting pandemonium.

The video went grainy as the helicopter must have sought

safety from a different position. Moments later the recording resumed, showing the armored truck barreling onto the scene. The HT was running toward it, and as the front passenger door swung open, bullets sprayed out of the back window at the law enforcement officers, who were returning fire. Dace watched as the gunman neared the moving vehicle, tossing the bags inside before reaching a hand to grasp the door handle. Then in the next moment he jerked as one leg crumpled, then the other. His grasp on the handle never loosened, but the vehicle was dragging him now, and Tyler rolled off his shoulders. A flak-vest-clad agent crawled over to grab the boy, pulling him to safety.

"We left the local SWAT snipers up there for additional coverage, and one had a better vantage point than our guys when this went down."

"Nice shot, Carter," Lewis said, satisfaction lacing his tone. Dace shot Ava a look of approval, and she inclined her head, her long dark hair swinging slightly. He felt a vicious stab of satisfaction that the only damn thing that had gone right in those few seconds could be attributed to their team.

He watched the TV screen as the rest of the drama unfolded. More shots were fired, and at least some of them hit their mark, before the HT was dragged into the vehicle as it sped away. A masked gunman leaned out the window and appeared to be shooting skyward, and the screen abruptly went blank.

"They ensured the media copter wouldn't follow them," observed Sanders.

"What about the boy? Tyler Mills."

Dace stilled at the sound of Jolie's voice. Details of the final minutes of the bank incident had succeeded in diverting his attention from the presence of the woman next to him, but his focus ricocheted back. Although he didn't look in her direction, he was supremely aware of the strain in her voice.

"He was taken to the hospital with lacerations and a concussion, but he should make a full recovery," Agent Dawson answered, speaking for the first time. "His mother was treated and released."

Dace sensed the tension creeping from her and moved his shoulders, impatient with himself. It was as if he were hyperaware around her, attuned to the slightest shift in her moods. Which was a joke, since he'd failed miserably at reading her during the last months they'd been together. Or maybe he'd been turned too inward to try. Hell, he didn't know. But he'd be damned if he'd allow her to walk back into his life and wield this kind of power the day she reentered it. The shock of seeing her again had knocked him off balance. He needed to regain his distance, fast.

"You've got the hospitals covered?" he asked. Not that he expected the HT's accomplices to risk having him treated in a hospital. As well prepared as they appeared to have been, they'd certainly know that medical professionals were required to report gunshot wounds.

"Of course. And from the amount of blood left behind, the gunman appears to be seriously wounded, so we got lucky there."

Luck hadn't had a damn thing to do with it. Ava Carter hadn't earned the call sign "Cold Shot" by chance.

"So including the HT, that brings the total team to at least three," Mendel surmised. "The driver, the shooter in the backseat and the hostage taker in the bank." Any one of them could have planned to pick up the explosive devices later, had they not been needed.

Fenholt used the remote to turn off the television. "Probably four or five," she said. "Even though an alert was on the airwaves within seconds of the truck pulling away, it was only spotted momentarily before we lost it for good.

Since it's hard to miss an armored vehicle, and one hasn't been found abandoned, we suspect they had a semi waiting nearby. The truck drove into its back, the semi pulled out." Almost as an afterthought she added, "But that's only a theory. We're also checking out all the buildings in a two-mile area surrounding the last sighting to be sure it isn't housed in a garage or warehouse."

Fenholt looked at Dr. Ryder, sitting a couple chairs down from Dace. "In the meantime, we need to focus on the conversations with the HT. What can we glean from them?"

"You've got the transcribed notes of the exchanges," he began.

"It's not enough." There was a snap in her voice, barely discernible, but there. The unflappable SAC was showing signs of stress. Dace wondered how much crap was raining down on her over this mess. "I want observations compiled from you and from the local HNT negotiators. Each of you will need to look over the transcript to see if it's complete before we turn it over to a forensic psychologist. In the meantime, is there anything that struck you about this guy that will help us in the short term?"

Meaning, of course, that what they had to offer was only valuable until her own people could support or dispute it. God save him from feds. Dace rubbed his jaw, faintly surprised by the scrape of beard against his palm. It was late and guaranteed to be later still before this was over. "He was educated." Their observations had been meticulously recorded and would have been included with the transcripts of the conversations. "A native English speaker. It seemed clear from the beginning that this wasn't about righting an imagined slight. He was there for the money."

"Obviously," Agent Hart put in from across the room. A few in the room chuckled tiredly.

"I mean we never got the impression that this was a disgruntled former customer or employee with a grievance that we could help resolve. And it's pretty clear from the preparation involved that these guys aren't amateurs. Especially if they're the same ones who have been hitting banks all over the state."

"That connection hasn't been established," Fenholt said flatly.

He gave her a sardonic smile. Whether it had been or not, this group wouldn't hear about it. The feds would wring the locals dry of every drop of relevant information and throw them crumbs in return. He was familiar with the way the game was played. "If there are two different crews working banks in the area, you've got a bigger problem than I thought."

"Like you say," put in Special Agent Truman, "it's *our* problem." His dislike for the man had nothing to do with his tone. That emotion had been instantaneous from the first time he'd shown up at the NOC unit.

"He's a loner." Dr. Ryder's matter-of-fact tone diffused some of the tension in the room. "He has trouble with authority figures, and with routine workdays in general. He may have a history of short-lived employment, possibly ending in altercations with his employers. Doesn't trust anyone except family."

"There was something in the notes about that." Fenholt tapped short-nailed fingers on the table as her gaze traveled around the table to land on Jolie. "The HT said something about 'seeing him soon.' But you didn't follow up on that line. Why is that? It seemed the opportune time, as you were discussing family."

The hint of censure in her voice elicited a familiar feeling in Dace, one that alarmed him enough to have him backpedaling wildly. He was long past the point when he should be feeling protective about Jolie. What she'd told the HT was true enough. She'd been orphaned as a child and had had only her grandmother growing up. Once the woman had died, Jolie had been on her own. And if there had been a time when he'd thought the three of them—he, Jolie and Sammy—were a family, well, that was in the distant past.

Something still compelled him to answer before Jolie had to. "You should have also read in the notes that the next contact with him was devoted to the preparations he was making with the hostages. From his remarks it was clear he was aware that your involvement meant limited time was left for negotiation. If we'd had more time to follow up—"

Agent Dawson interrupted him. "It's apparent from the well-orchestrated rescue attempt that the gunman was merely biding his time. The end result was a given as soon as a police response arrived at the bank. He wouldn't have been aware of any tactical preparations we were making. He was completely cut off from all outside communication other than the throw phone."

Looking at the faces of the other local law enforcement in the room, Dace realized he wasn't the only one who saw the flaw in the man's reasoning. "His accomplices were well aware of how things were progressing, though. Someone had to be close enough to monitor the situation and signal him somehow that things were about to go down." From the closed expressions of the agents in the room, it was clear that he wasn't going to get any response to that statement. Catching Chief Sanders's eye, he scowled, but sat back in his seat, saying nothing further. He'd never acquired a taste for jumping through the fed's hoops.

"Our interest in your observations is limited to your conversations with the HT." Fenholt pulled the bound notes toward her and took a pair of bifocals from her jacket pocket, settling them on her nose. Flipping to the first page, she studied it for a moment before looking up. "You indicated you didn't notice an accent. What about word choice?"

Once again Jolie answered, as if not trusting what response Dace would make. Maybe that meant she was as attuned to him as he was to her. He had a few choice words for Fenholt and her team, although he knew better than to utter them.

Like what were the chances they could have learned more—a lot more—if the feds hadn't rushed the response along to a tactical conclusion? Could those three lives have been saved? It wasn't a question that seemed to dog Fenholt. But he knew it would haunt him for a long time to come.

It was after midnight when Jolie wearily pulled her car to a stop in a parking space in front of her rented condo unit. The darkness was kinder to the condominium complex than daylight was, hiding the blistered paint, sagging eaves and loose porch railing. It was the best she'd been able to find on such short notice. She'd resigned her job with the LAPD, sought reinstatement with the Metro City PD and then moved, all within a matter of weeks.

In the intervening time she'd had plenty of opportunity to regret her decision, but none more so than today.

She opened the glove compartment and stashed her wallet and cell phone inside, locking it before getting out of her car, securing the door with the remote. It wasn't that she hadn't expected to run into Dace at some point. Although she had planned to avoid the hangouts they'd frequented with friends from the department, it would have been only a matter of time before she would have encountered him.

Trudging up the steps, she fit her key into the dead bolt of her door. But somehow she'd expected to have more time to prepare herself. More time to make sure her defenses were firmly in place.

And, honesty forced her to admit, she'd hoped that the time they'd spent apart had suffocated any feelings she might have once had for him. God knew she'd done everything she could to stomp out those lingering emotions.

There had been men in the intervening time, of course. First to fill that painful void inside her, and when that failed, enough of them to assure herself that she'd regained her former famous detachment. And it had worked admirably. None of them had made her feel a thing.

Yet it had taken only the sound of Dace's voice, the sight of him again, to summon that familiar tangle of emotion that still tightened her chest, strangled her breathing and caused all the pulses in her body to throb.

It was the stress of seeing him for the first time, coupled with the strain from today's incident and debriefing. She told herself that and almost believed it. There would be no reason for that to recur, as she'd be requesting a reassignment to the other HNT squad as soon as possible.

A pang shot through her. It was highly probable that another assignment wouldn't be available. But she couldn't worry about that. She agreed with Dace on one thing—she was no more eager to see him at every incident than he was her.

Pushing the door open, she stepped inside, mentally steeling herself. The apartment was dark. Quiet. But the scent of cigarettes stung the air. Anxiety was already prickling her skin when a familiar querulous voice split the shadows.

"Where you been? I could starve around here. I'm supposed to be getting regular meals. Not that you care."

Anxiety melted away and old defenses slammed into place. "If you haven't eaten, it's your own fault. I've got a tab set up for you at the restaurant around the corner. You know that."

"Well, they don't got Mexican, do they? I was in the mood for enchiladas all day. You leave me here without two cents to rub together like I was some kind of slave or something."

Jolie snapped on a lamp to reveal her mother sitting in the armchair she favored in the corner of the room. It used to face a TV, but that had disappeared the first day Jolie had reported for work with the MCPD, along with the microwave and stereo equipment. She had wised up quickly. Everything else of value had been put in storage so Trixie couldn't sell or trade it for something to get her high.

"Unlike slaves, you're free to leave anytime." Aware of the edge in her tone, she made an effort to soften it. "I'll make something to eat. Didn't you get the message I left on the answering machine? I had to respond to an incident today and I never had a chance to—"

"The least you could do is to buy some decent groceries." Trixie stabbed out the cigarette she wasn't supposed to be smoking in an ashtray. "All that green stuff gives me the trots."

Jolie's temples began to throb. "Vegetables are especially good for your condition. Dr. Baxter said—"

"He's a quack." Trixie tapped the cigarette package against the table, selected another cigarette. Since Jolie made sure Trixie never had any money of her own, she could only assume that her mother had shoplifted them. Another of her endearing habits. "I ain't going back to him no more anyway."

"Your choice." Jolie would never be sure what had made her overcome a lifetime of distrust and ambivalence to rescue her mother from her own excesses. Whatever it was, it didn't extend to false sympathy. "You know your options as well as I do."

Dodging the smoke ring floating her way, she unstrapped her weapon and locked it in the gun safe. Then she headed

toward the kitchen. Since she needed fuel, she'd cook something and Trixie could eat or not, as she wished. It was useless
to try to argue with her. The woman had spent her life avoid-
ing responsibility for anything or anyone, including herself.
It was hard to work up empathy now that Trixie's past had
caught up with her.

Without a microwave it took twice as much time as it
should have taken to thaw chicken breasts and put a simple
meal together. Serving up the dinner on two plates, she took
one to the sullen older woman and sat it on the end table next
to her, going back to eat at the countertop island.

"My mother teach you to cook like this? Good thing I let
you stay with her some. Learned something useful." Trixie
sawed at the meat and popped a piece into her mouth,
chewing vigorously with her remaining teeth.

"Gran died when I was eight," Jolie replied tightly. And
she was grateful for the time she'd spent with the older
woman, who'd given her the only real home she'd ever had.
But she'd learned to cook at her fifth—or was it sixth?—
foster home. Of all the lessons learned while she was passed
from one foster family to another like unwanted baggage,
cooking had been by far the most useful.

They ate in silence then. Jolie finished first and got up to
rinse her plate and put it in the dishwasher. She made no move
to collect Trixie's. One of the ground rules she'd set before
allowing her mother to move in with her was that she pick
up after herself, at least as long as she was able to.

The cancer that was ravaging Trixie's body was just finishing the job her high-risk lifestyle had started thirty years
earlier. A lifetime ago, before Jolie had been old enough to
truly understand who and what her mother was, the thought
of living with her—like a real family—had been a little girl's
fantasy. This was the reality. She'd learned the hard way

that dreams were just that. Life was far from perfect. Far from easy.

She checked the clock, nearly groaned when she saw that it was past one-thirty. If she went to bed now she'd be lucky to get five hours' sleep before reporting for duty tomorrow. "I'm going to turn in."

"Wait a minute. I've been sitting here alone all day. The least you can do is talk to me." Trixie wiped her mouth on the napkin Jolie had given her, then tossed it on her now-empty plate.

Guilt warring with exhaustion, Jolie hesitated. Unless Trixie chose to go out to eat or for a walk, there was absolutely nothing for her to do. Her fault, of course, since she'd traded the TV and stereo for ready cash, but still... In that position Jolie knew she'd go stark raving mad inside a week.

"I could pick up some more magazines for you tomorrow." She sank down on the arm of the sofa, surveying her mother. "Did you finish the ones I brought home before?"

Trixie waved a hand. "I ain't never been much for reading. I think what I need is to get out more. Get some fresh air. That's what Dr. Baxter said, remember?"

The man Trixie had earlier denounced as a quack. Instantly wary, Jolie said noncommittally, "I remember."

"What I've been thinking about is going to the beach." She lit another cigarette and crossed one skeletally thin leg over the other, causing her too short skirt to ride up past the point of modesty, if Trixie had ever possessed any. "The sound of the ocean. The fresh breeze coming in off the sea. 'Member when I used to take you to the beach when you was little?"

"No." Jolie refused to join in the pretense. The only places she'd ever gone with Trixie had been to dive taverns and dilapidated apartments occupied by dealers who sold whatever it was Trixie was using at the time.

But that wasn't quite right. There had been that little field trip to the police station when Trixie had been slapped with her third soliciting charge, while Jolie had been stashed in the backseat of a car parked nearby.

"Well, I did," Trixie snapped. "All the time. Now, I know you gotta work. But I was thinking about it since this friend of mine, Claudia—I don't think you ever met her—I ran into her the other day. Asked me if I wanted to take a trip along the Coastal Highway and I thought, 'Why not?' I might as well enjoy the time I got left, right?"

Jolie didn't answer. She was waiting for the shakedown. Trixie had it mastered to an art form.

The older woman finished her cigarette and immediately lit another. "'Course, I wouldn't feel right going along and not paying for nothing. There's gas money and I'd need a little for meals. Couple nights in a motel." She snuck a peek at Jolie through the haze of smoke. "Wouldn't be too much. A couple hundred dollars would do it, probably. I could be back Sunday."

"No." Jolie got up and headed toward her room.

"You're a selfish bitch, you know that?" Trixie's voice went from pleasant to ugly with a speed a starlet would envy. There was a loud crash. Jolie said a silent goodbye to the woman's plate. "Who are you to tell me I can't have a little fun, huh? You got the money. I know you do."

Jolie turned, noting the shards of broken stoneware on the far side of the room before facing her mother. Trixie was breathing hard, her expression twisted in a snarl. "That's right, I do. But I'm not giving it to you, because I know your idea of fun goes up your nose. I've told you before, I'll give you a place to live. Feed you. Clothe you. Line up medical assistance. But I won't help you kill yourself." Her lips curved humorlessly. "You've always done an admirable job of that on your own." She started for her bedroom, more in a hurry than ever to put an end to this day.

"That kid of yours is better off dead, with you as a mother." Jolie froze, battling back the unexpected wave of agony that was never far away. After thrusting the verbal dagger, Trixie twisted it. "Lucky it never had to grow up and deal with you. You're pure ice, through and through. Don't give a damn about anyone but yourself."

It took a moment for her lungs to ease. Another for the power of speech to return. Fighting to surface from the tide of anguish, Jolie shot the woman a look over her shoulder. "If that's true, you must be really proud. I learned from a master, didn't I?" Spine rigid, she turned and walked down the hall to her bedroom, closing the door behind her quietly.

"Fix him."

At the order, the intern, Clark Howard, glanced up from his ministrations to the unconscious man. He didn't like the hard, set expression on the second man's face. He liked the gun pointing at his head even less.

"I've tried. But he's lost too much blood. One of the bullets nicked his femoral artery. Infection has set in in the right leg. He needs to get to a hospital. It's his only chance." A very slim one, at this point.

"Wrong," came the soft reply. "*You're* his only chance. And he's yours. Because if he dies, so do you."

Twenty-four hours ago Clark might have believed that. But then twenty-four hours ago he'd believed he was doing the right thing by cutting his smoking break short outside the hospital to run to the stranger's aid as he yelled for help from a nearby car.

But now he knew better. He'd been a sucker. He'd seen some of the newscasts about the bank robbery and he could guess who his patient was. Regardless of the outcome in this room, his own death had been certain even before he'd been yanked inside that car. Even before it had sped away.

"We got you everything you said." The second man indicated the mound of medicine, bandages and surgical equipment. "You can do anything the hospital can."

Clark swallowed a wave of frustration. "He needs IV fluids, heavy-duty antibiotics, a CT and possibly an amputation. I can't do any of that."

The man's gaze shifted for a moment to the patient, and Clark thought he saw a flicker of indecision in his expression. Pressing the point, he rose and began talking rapidly. "Listen, you can drop us both off at the hospital. I'll see him safely in. No one will have to know about you. About this."

There was a moment, a brief instant when he thought he'd won a reprieve. When he believed the second man would do the right thing, the thing Clark had been begging him to do since he'd gotten pulled into that car.

Then the patient made a gurgling sound, and Clark froze for a moment before dropping to his knees beside him again to check for vitals. But the death rattle had heralded the patient's demise, and, Clark realized, his own.

He administered CPR more as an avoidance than anything else. The man with the gun was still. So still. When the intern finally rocked back on his heels, sweating and afraid, he raised his gaze reluctantly and saw exactly what he'd expected.

"Wait." He swallowed hard, hands out in supplication. "You have to realize—"

The shot to the middle of his forehead left his sentence unfinished.

The gunman kicked the intern's body aside to kneel down next to that of his little brother, the brother he'd been looking after one way or another all his life. Grief welled, was ruthlessly pushed aside. Grief solved nothing. Sorrow was weakness, and this wasn't a time to be weak.

Fury flared then, and he fanned the embers, welcoming the hot lick of rage igniting nerve endings, firing a thirst for revenge.

The death of David John Marker wouldn't go unavenged. He'd make sure they paid.

Every damn one of them.

Chapter 5

She could change jobs, change locations, but one constant remained. Monday mornings sucked. Nothing ever seemed to change that.

Jolie unlocked the gun safe, took out her holstered weapon and quickly strapped it on. She was running later than she'd like, mostly because the stress of a weekend spent with Trixie hadn't been conducive to restful nights.

It was impossible to keep the woman amused given that all her favorite pastimes were illegal or immoral. By Sunday Jolie had felt like she was dealing with a badly behaved hyperactive three-year-old. In a fit of desperation, she'd gone shopping for another TV. The puzzled salesperson had assured her that it could be chained to the wall, much like they were in motels. The service would cost her another couple hundred dollars, but hopefully it would stop her mother from letting one of her low-life friends into the apartment to help himself to Jolie's things in exchange for favors she didn't even want to consider.

She grabbed her purse and stepped over to take another look at the calendar. Trixie's next visit with the oncologist was Friday, and she made a mental note to tell her lieutenant she'd be taking a few hours off. Her mother couldn't be trusted to relay the doctor's advice, or even to keep the appointment on her own.

The knock at the front door had her jerking around, startled. The TV wasn't due to be delivered until tomorrow, and it was too early for visitors, not that she'd had any since she moved back. She was reluctant to explain Trixie to any of her friends. It struck her then that the only "guests" entertained in the apartment since she'd acquired it were the ones Trixie had invited to carry off Jolie's electronics. The irony didn't escape her.

The knocking was repeated, louder this time. She strode to the door, not anxious for Trixie to awaken. But when she checked the peephole, her legs went to water.

She slapped one hand on the doorjamb for support. Dace filled the small opening. Big. Unsmiling. Larger than life. Much as he'd filled her life, once upon a time.

Jolie slammed the figurative door on that memory and opened the literal one before her.

"What do you want?"

His brows skimmed upward. "Still a morning person, I see."

She took a breath, strove for an impassive mask to match his. "I'm running a little late. You can talk on the way to my car." Without waiting for a response, she stepped out, pulling the door shut behind her.

But Dace stood in place eyeing the condominium complex, with its ill-kept shrubs and peeling paint. "You need to talk to the landlord about your maintenance agreement. Seems like he's falling down on the job a bit."

The daylight did the place no favors. She didn't bother to tell him the inside was only slightly better than the exterior. Or that she had lived in far worse in her life. "I'll do that."

He slipped his hands in the pockets of his dark trousers as he strolled along with her. He was wearing a matching black shirt, muted tie and shoulder harness. He must have left his jacket in his vehicle. There was a fresh nick on his chin, courtesy of his morning shave. Noticing it had a ball of nerves tightening in her stomach.

"Why are you here?"

"You didn't answer your cell."

She looked at him blankly. The cell was in her glove box, along with her wallet. So far the precautions had kept them out of Trixie's clutches. "And you called my cell because…"

"Not me. Lewis. The feds have called a meeting for this morning. He was in a hurry, so when he told me he couldn't reach you I said I'd swing by. He gave me the address and…" He shrugged, the familiar gesture striking a chord in her.

His explanation didn't make sense. "He has my landline number. Why didn't he try that?"

"Said it wasn't working."

She frowned, halting to look back at her apartment door. That was odd. The phone had worked fine yesterday, when she'd called the electronics store to see when they were open. Then she'd been gone a couple hours to buy the TV….

She closed her eyes, a grim sense of certainty filling her. Maybe there was a malfunction. That was possible.

It was also possible that Trixie had gotten her hands on a little cash in Jolie's absence yesterday by pawning the telephone/answering machine to her friends. And Jolie had been stressed enough that she hadn't even missed it.

She checked her watch, debating whether she had time to go back inside to check. "What time is the meeting?"

"Eight. We just have time to make it."

Annoyed, she turned her back on the apartment and resumed walking. "Have there been developments in the investigation?" If so, it would be unusual for the feds to share them with the locals. She had figured that the debriefing the previous week would be their last direct involvement in the case.

"Lewis wouldn't say. But I heard something that I think explains the urgency." He stopped, turning to face her. Jolie was struck by his grim expression. "Ava Carter was shot as she was going into a grocery store Saturday afternoon."

Her throat abruptly dried. "Did she... Was she..."

"She's alive and her condition has stabilized. No word on the shooter. But that, coupled with Lewis's call this morning makes me think the feds want to discuss whether it could possibly be connected to the case."

Everything inside her rejected the idea. "You've got a suspicious mind. More likely they've got a preliminary profile from their agency shrink and want to run it by us."

"Yeah, because they hold our opinion in such high esteem." She shot him an amused glance. She'd always enjoyed his sardonic outlook, since she wasn't exactly a Pollyanna herself. They'd connected first through the job they shared, with passion following quickly. And then... She swallowed hard, forcing her gaze to the parking lot ahead of them. Sammy had forged a bond between them that couldn't be broken, couldn't be outdistanced. Even now his ghost loomed, silent and somehow reproachful.

"You're going to have a heckuva time backing your car out." Dace squinted at her dated sedan. He'd tried to get her to trade it when they'd been together, but she'd refused. She had no interest in cars, and as long as hers still ran and parts weren't falling off, it was good enough.

She followed his gaze across the parking lot and irritation rose. "Some drunk with a depth-perception problem must have decided to take his space and part of mine, too." A non-descript white sedan hugged her car on the passenger side, the door handles nearly touching. How was she ever going to get out of the space without hooking its mirror with her own?

Surveying the position of the vehicles, she decided she could pull straight ahead over the curb without touching the other vehicle, if she was extremely careful. Her Monday-morning mood went from peevish to surly. She was tempted to hunt down the driver and kick his ass, whether it made her late to work or not.

"Listen to me, Jolie."

The quiet urgency in Dace's voice managed to distract her from her violent thoughts. "You can think I'm paranoid, fine, but when I say go, you're going to turn and run like hell. Ready?"

She scowled at him, at a loss. "Why should I…"

His hand gripped her elbow tightly. "Go!" He abruptly turned, yanking her with him and half dragging her across the lot back in the direction they'd come. "Stay down!" he yelled, running in a crouch, never loosening his grasp.

She ran. She didn't have a choice. In a heartbeat, the focus of her ire switched from the driver of the sedan to the man beside her. "You idiot, what are you—"

The explosion drowned out her protest, the impact knocking them off their feet and propelling them through the air. When they landed, amid a shower of debris, Jolie's head bounced hard against something solid. Then everything went black.

* * *

"What the hell do you think you're doing?"

Adam Marker listened to the barely controlled anger in the caller's voice as he flipped through the news stations with the remote. "Any update on Conrad's status? I can't find a thing on TV yet." Damn reporters were always sticking their noses in everywhere, except when you actually needed them.

"Marker, listen to me. You're out of control. You're going to bring this whole thing down on all of us. You start trying to assassinate police officers, and the world begins crashing in pretty damn quick."

"The update, Gee." The caller went silent at the use of the hated nickname. "That was your job. Is Conrad dead?"

A long hesitation. Then, "No. My source at the hospital says she hasn't regained consciousness yet. Recker walked away with only a few scratches."

Fury flared, a lit match to a gasoline-soaked fuse. The remote sailed across the room, shattering the television screen. "Sonuvabitch!" It had seemed like fate to see Recker pull up outside Conrad's apartment this morning. David would have called it a two-fer. Two dead cops with one explosion.

But neither had died. He'd planned so carefully. A car bomb activated by the car's ignition could be detonated too soon by a remote starting device. And he'd been afraid a cop would be cautious enough to check the chassis for IEDs.

But he hadn't been smart enough. Rage hazed his vision. Another failure, like Carter, who had escaped death only because she'd stopped her approach to the grocery store to dig for her cell phone in her purse.

Lucky. All three of them. And why did they deserve luck when it had deserted his brother?

"I know you're devastated over David's death." The low soothing tone came from the cell Marker had almost forgotten he was holding. "You want revenge. That's understandable. You can still have it. But not now. Not with every law enforcement agency in the area hunting for us. Get out of the state. Lie low a while. Start planning our next job. That's what you do best, remember? The planning."

Marker stared blankly at the ruined TV, not seeing it. Yeah, he'd been the brains. David had been the weapons expert. If it had been David using a car bomb, or with the rifle, there would be three dead cops right now.

And if it had been Adam lying in a shallow grave up in the hills instead of his brother, his death would already be avenged. That certainty haunted him. Kept him awake nights cursing a god he'd never believed in. David wouldn't have let Gee prevent him from doing what was right. What was *just*. He wouldn't have run and hidden.

And neither would Adam. "No," he said hoarsely.

"They'll be easier targets later, once all this dies down. When the cops go back to their dreary lives, let their guard down again, it'll be like picking off ducks in a row."

"I said no. We do this my way. And you'll do what you're told because we both know what you stand to lose." Tension stretched like a thrumming wire between them. "But you're right about one thing. I need to plan. The next attempt has to be fatal. And you're going to help make that happen…."

The quiet rhythmic beeping filtered through Jolie's subconscious. Awareness returned sluggishly. Comprehension was slower to follow. She felt heavy. Weighted down. It was a struggle to shrug off the heavy blanket of unconsciousness that even now was sucking her back into oblivion.

Fighting the feeling, she concentrated on the sounds around her. The beeping. A hissing noise. A slight rattling.

Other sensations registered. She was in a bed. Voices sounded in the distance, jumbled and muted. There was a faint smell of antiseptic.

A hospital.

Wincing, she tried to open her eyes. She hated hospitals. When she found out who was responsible for putting her here, she'd tear a strip off them. Struggling to sit upright, she closed her eyes again when they refused to focus. She wasn't staying here. The only time she'd stayed overnight in the hospital was when she'd had…

"Sammy." The word escaped in a whimper as her head started a vicious clamoring that had her gritting her teeth, grabbing the side rail for support.

"For God's sakes, lie down."

Her eyes popped open at the brusque tone. Three Dace Reckers swam in her vision. She blinked and only two remained, both wavering at the edges until they melded into one. He loomed over her bedside, close. Too close. She obeyed his command only to shut out his image.

With her head resting against the pillow again, his appearance registered belatedly. He looked like he'd been in a fight. She frowned. He hadn't been a brawler while they'd been together, but maybe he'd developed a bad habit in the time since. He had a black eye, and there was a nasty scratch along his jawline.

Her gaze traveled over him. He was dressed in a short-sleeved navy T-shirt and jeans. A long ugly scrape marred his forearm and his palm had a large square patch of gauze over it.

"What happened to you?"

He eyed her carefully. "Don't you remember?"

Jolie searched her memory banks, came up blank. "I...I remember you coming to my apartment this morning."

"That was yesterday."

Yesterday. What the hell had happened? She closed her eyes, reaching for elusive snippets of memory. What had he been doing at her place? Something about a meeting. Her cell. The car.

Fragments of memory swirled in a mental jumble. She waited for the pieces to settle. She recalled walking to the parking lot with him. The stupid driver who had parked practically on top of her car. Her irritation, and then Dace shoving her, forcing her to flee.

Her eyes popped open. "Car bomb?"

He nodded, his expression grim. "Maybe it was because of Ava getting shot, but that car parked practically on top of yours gave me an itchy feeling."

"Lucky for me," she said faintly.

"Yeah. Lucky."

She wondered at the bleakness in his tone, but then her attention splintered. Scowling, she demanded, "How come I'm in a hospital bed and you aren't?"

A slight smirk settled on his lips. "I don't like hospitals."

"Neither do I." She struggled to a sitting position again, ignoring his protest, and fumbled for the button to raise the head of the bed. "Get the doctor. I'm leaving."

He made no motion to obey. "You're not going anywhere. You hit your head and when you came to you were putting up such a fight they had to restrain you in order to check you over."

"Yeah, well, I don't like doctors either." She shrugged, winced when the action brought pain. She must have bruised more than her head. Looking herself over critically, she found no bandages on her arms, except for a piece of tape keeping an IV in place. She moved her legs under the sheet testingly. There was a chorus of aches, but apparently nothing broken. She was fine.

Jolie said as much, but her words did nothing to ease the concern from Dace's expression. "The feds are outside. Been haunting this place since they heard the news. They're wanting to talk to you."

"I don't know why. You probably told them everything I could."

"I did."

"Well, then, what's—"

The door pushed open and Special Agents Dawson and Truman appeared. "We heard voices." Dawson's gaze was assessing as it raked over Jolie. "Detective Conrad. How are you feeling?"

"Fine." She was starting to feel like a parrot. Surreptitiously she tugged the sheet higher over her thin cotton hospital gown, hating the sense of vulnerability that came from her position.

Both agents surprised her by pulling up chairs close to the bed and sitting down. "You're very fortunate." Dawson's glance took in Dace, too. "Both of you. The bomb squad examined the explosive that blew the car. It was remote detonated, just like the ones found at the bank site. Trigger device, which means…"

"…that the trigger man had to be in the vicinity," Jolie finished softly. Her arms prickled at the thought of someone watching her as she approached the car. Waiting for her to draw close enough to kill. Swallowing hard, she forced her tone to remain steady. "Cell-phone triggers are a lot more common these days."

Dawson and Truman exchanged a look. Dace's expression grew cloudier. Dawson said, "The explosives at the bank site weren't triggered by cell phones either. I suspect the subjects knew we'd take out the cell-phone grid to prevent outside communication with the guy inside. We have reason to believe you were targeted by one of the bank robber's accomplices. The day Carter got shot we discovered the identities of the responding SWAT squad and affiliated personnel were posted on a Web site inciting violence against law enforcement officials."

The news had Jolie feeling weaker than she had since she'd recovered consciousness. "Killcop.com?" Her gaze swung to Dace, and she saw her answer in his expression. "We're on Killcop?"

"We've already successfully pursued an injunction and got the information pulled," Dawson said quickly. "But these sites are pervasive. Shut one down and three more spring up to take its place. They take on a life of their own."

She knew that was true. The site advocating a stop to snitching had incited nothing less than a cultural revolution in some inner-city neighborhoods, making police work there doubly difficult. When no one was willing to tell what they saw, violent criminals walked.

And when police were identified to all, retaliation was violent and increasingly frequent.

"You suspected Ava's shooting was connected," she said to Dace. That morning—yesterday?—she'd scoffed at his suspicion, but it had saved both of their lives.

"I had a hunch," he explained tersely when both agents looked at him. "Which turned out to be lucky as hell, since you left us in the dark about the link."

Truman spoke for the first time. "Ballistics matched the slugs taken from Carter with bullets from outside the bank. And now of course with the similarities in the explosives we can verify our suppositions."

"Glad to know that us nearly getting blown to hell and back could help you guys out," Dace retorted.

Truman's bulldog jaw tightened, but Dawson said smoothly, "I understand your concern. The meeting that took place yesterday morning was to alert everyone to be doubly careful. Unfortunately, the warning came too late for you two."

Jolie shook her head. The logic of their reasoning still escaped her. "This doesn't make sense. The HT got away with nearly a million dollars. There's a massive manhunt for them. Why wouldn't they have headed out of state?"

"This is one theory," Dawson said, smoothing the crease of his immaculate trousers. "It is possible that the HT died from his injuries. He lost a lot of blood at the scene. And an intern from a nearby hospital disappeared while on his break the same day as the bank robbery—he could have been grabbed to treat the HT. If the HT died, his death could be the motivation for the accomplices to seek revenge."

The headache Jolie had awakened with intensified. It felt as if a dozen demented gnomes were jackhammering in her temples. For the first time she thought of Trixie. A ball of nerves clutched in her stomach. What was the woman doing without Jolie there to keep her in line? Did she even know what had occurred?

She slid a glance at Dace. No way was she going to broach the subject while he was in the room. "Was there damage to the condominium complex across from my parking lot?"

"Some blown windows," Truman answered. "Most of the vehicles nearby were destroyed."

The news allayed some of her unease. But she still needed out of here. The longer she left Trixie unattended the less likely it was she'd have an apartment to return to.

Determinedly, she stabbed a finger at the call button on the side of the bed. When a disembodied voice answered, presumably from the nurse's station, Jolie said, "Get a doctor in here. I'm leaving within the hour, with or without a release."

Dawson frowned. "I don't think that's—"

"The hell you are." Dace's voice overrode the agent's. "You'll wait until they give you the okay. You aren't going to do anyone any good running around with a head injury."

"An hour. Then I'm out of here." To the agents she said, "So what was the official recommendation at the debriefing we missed? Wear Kevlar and take bikes to work?" She managed, barely, to keep her sarcasm in check.

Dawson spoke. "We've conferred with your superiors. Naturally, they're concerned about their squad members walking around as possible targets."

Dace made a rude sound and Jolie sent him a warning look. "Naturally."

"I believe the personnel involved have been instructed to be extra cautious, both on the job and off it."

"Chief of Police Sanders is suggesting everyone consider taking any leave they have accumulated," Dace added. "Advice that you should follow."

His words brought a pang. He'd made no bones about his desire to see the end of her since they'd been partnered up. But what he was suggesting was impossible.

Trixie's doctor was here. And for whatever reason, the woman refused to leave the area. Jolie had tried everything to convince her to come live with her in LA, before eventually giving up and moving back here. If she was going to stick it out with the woman, it had to be in Metro City.

"Actually…" The slight hesitation in Agent Dawson's voice had her interest sharpening. He leaned forward, his expression urgent. "Special Agent Fenholt believes it might be helpful if one of your squad maintained some sort of visibility. With our protection, of course."

"No."

Jolie threw a glare at Dace, before flicking a glance at Truman. He was watching her impassively. Returning her attention to Dawson, she said warily, "Let me guess. You want to draw the accomplice out."

"He's a threat." Dawson's tone, the somber expression on his coffee-colored face were persuasive. "Not only to the banks and unsuspecting customers, but to every member on your response unit. Right now he's focused on revenge, and that could keep him in the area long enough for us to nail him."

"You are out of your freakin' mind." Dace surged to his feet, fists knotted. "You want to use her as bait? Dangle her out there and wait for this lunatic to try again?"

"He hasn't made an attempt against a man yet," Truman put in. "Maybe because he sees the female officers as more vulnerable, maybe because Carter and Conrad were two of the members most closely involved with the HT, he went after them first."

She swallowed. Most closely involved. You could say that. Ava Carter had probably killed the man and Jolie had been the one talking to him a great deal of the time prior to that. Did this accomplice blame her for not preventing the outcome? Or was the chief right, and every member of the squad was at risk?

"She's not going to be your sacrificial lamb," Dace said flatly. "Think of something else."

Her attention fractured. He'd always had this take-charge mentality, she recalled, and they'd gone a round or two over it in the past. His protectiveness had annoyed and touched her by turn, but mostly it had baffled her. For someone used to making

her own way and looking out for herself, it had been difficult
to adjust to taking someone else's feelings into consideration.

But that was when their situation had given him some say
in her decisions. That time was long over.

"Carter is recovering nicely," Dawson pressed. "We made
the proposition to her, but unfortunately she has a son depend-
ing on her."

And you have no one.

The unspoken words hung in the air, little shards of jagged
glass that could slice at her heart if she let them. Reaching
for the cloak of professionalism, she shoved aside emotion
and concentrated on the matter at hand.

They didn't know about Trixie, of course. How could
they? She'd only reentered her life—Jolie had only *allowed*
her into her life—a few weeks ago. And her prognosis was
dismal. In just a few weeks or months hospice would take
over much of Jolie's obligation.

The three dead cops had probably had families. Wives.
Children. Not to mention the bank's security guard. Until the
subjects were stopped, more casualties would pile up.

This time, one of those casualties had almost been a two-
year-old boy.

"You can't seriously be considering this." Dace's voice
was low. Controlled. But she could hear the fury just below
the surface. "They're playing you. Using your dedication to
the job to justify putting yourself in danger."

She gave him a distracted glance. He could be persuasive.
Hadn't he once convinced her to set aside every shred of
common sense, every well-defined defense to take a chance
on a family of sorts? Maybe those skills were what made him
so successful as a negotiator. But he wouldn't be allowed to
undermine her judgment again.

"I'd like to talk to the agents alone."

His eyes widened fractionally. "I know what you're think-ing. Better than anyone else could. Don't do this, Jolie. It would be for all the wrong reasons."

"You heard her, Recker." There was an unmistakably smug sound to Truman's voice. "She wants you out of here."

But he didn't budge. Stubbornness had been another of his unswerving traits. His gaze never left hers, and there was a moment, just an instant, when the intensity in his green eyes nearly undid her determination.

So she forced herself to look away. Strove for a steel in her words that she was far from feeling. "It's my decision. I'll make it alone."

Silence hung in the air, brittle with fragility. The moment stretched, the quiet underscoring the rattle of the blinds as the air-conditioning unit turned on, the hiss and beep of the IV machine.

Finally, after what seemed an eternity, Dace moved away from the bed. Crossed the room. Went out the door. And somehow the sight of him walking away brought an all-too-familiar hollowness to her chest.

"You're making the right choice here, Jolie. SAC Fenholt thinks this could be our best chance to catch this guy."

With effort, she forced her gaze away from the closed door and to Special Agent Dawson's earnest expression. "I haven't agreed to anything yet. I have a few conditions that need to be met." With a sense of grim satisfaction she noted the wariness that crossed the agent's face. "First I run this by Chief Sanders. See where he stands on it."

"I can assure you, the chief has been fully apprised of our suggestion."

"You'll excuse me if I want to hear his take myself," she said dryly.

"Okay." With success in sight, Dawson was all agreeableness. "You'll talk to Sanders. Let me tell you what SAC Fenholt has planned—"

"That's not all. I'm caring for my—" it was still hard to say the word "—mother, who's terminally ill. She can't stay in the condominium. He knows where I live, and it will be easy enough to find out about her, too. He might try to strike at me through her."

The two agents exchanged a look. "We didn't know about her," Truman muttered.

If this wasn't so damn hard, she might have enjoyed his chagrin. "I'll only agree if she's protected, too. Someone has to take her to her doctor's appointments…"

Their expressions grew pained.

"…and she really can't be left alone. She doesn't need nursing care yet, but she does have to be watched. Carefully." What Trixie would make of all this, Jolie didn't want to consider. Again she was struck with a compulsion to get out of there and find out for herself.

"All right." Dawson's tone was clipped, not nearly as smooth as it had been earlier. "Anything else?"

"That will be plenty," she said dryly. Once they met Trixie, she was certain they'd agree.

"All right. We'll get started on the arrangements. Now let me tell you what we have in mind."

The door pushed open. The doctor, and about time. "Later. We'll talk details after I speak to the chief."

But the man wasn't alone. Dace was right behind him. And with one quick encompassing look at the room's occupants, he seemed to size up the conversation that had taken place in his absence.

"I hear you're in a hurry to leave us," the doctor said in a harried voice, looking at her chart as spoke.

Dace stared at Jolie. "You're going to do this?"

"My decision. My business."

He gave a short nod. "Yeah." His attention switched to the agents, who were rising from their chairs. "The way I figure it, two sacrificial lambs are better than one."

A chair scraped the floor as Dawson pushed it out of the way. The doctor jockeyed around the trio of men, trying to get to Jolie's side.

Truman folded his arms across his chest. "What are you saying, Recker?"

But Jolie had followed his meaning all too easily. Irritation rose, mixed with an inexplicable measure of panic. "No, Dace. That's not necessary."

He answered Truman as if she hadn't spoken. "I'm saying Jolie isn't going to be left hanging out there by herself. If she does this, so do I."

Chapter 6

"Absolutely not."

Dace ignored the vehemence in Jolie's tone and addressed the agents. "Why don't we step outside and give the doctor and patient some privacy?"

"I was just going to suggest that myself," the doctor said. "Out. Everybody."

"Dawson, don't listen to him." Dace accompanied the feds to the door, Jolie's words trailing behind him. "We've already got a viable plan. We don't need him." He pulled the door shut behind them and left Jolie to the doctor's ministrations. Her words resonated.

Certainly she'd never needed him on any level that mattered. His jaw tightened. He'd thought she did, at one time. He'd believed that circumstances had linked them in a way that couldn't be denied. But then Sammy had died. What had been between them had withered. She'd walked out without a second glance, proving him dead wrong.

Yet here he was again, voluntarily aligning himself with her, when he knew all he was going to get for his efforts was a kick in the teeth.

Except this time was going to be different. *He* was different. This had nothing to do with Jolie personally, and everything to do with the job. He wouldn't hang any of his partners out to dry, and if she was bound and determined to go ahead with this thing, then he had no choice but to stick with her. The feds didn't inspire a lot of faith. He could recite chapter and verse the times when something like this went to hell. He wasn't going to leave a fellow officer alone with a target on her forehead, even if that officer was stubborn enough to defy all logic.

Even if that officer was Jolie.

A murmur of voices drifted from the hospital room before he heard Jolie's voice raised in argument. He knew her well enough to be certain that the encounter wasn't going to improve her mood. Under the circumstances, he couldn't spare her any sympathy.

From Agent Dawson's expression, Dace could tell that the man was inclined to agree with Jolie's assessment, so he started talking fast. "There's no way to be sure the bank team will stick around and try again. They've failed twice to take out a member of the SWAT unit. Things will be heating up for them as a result of the investigation. What we have to do is present them with an opportunity they can't resist. Move Jolie in with me."

He watched the two agents look at each other. "There's a problem with that suggestion, Recker," Truman put in. "Conrad doesn't want you in on this with her."

There was a burn in his chest at the truth, but Dace didn't focus on it. Not then. "Well, she's not calling the shots on this, is she? For whatever reason, she's up for the assignment. So am

I. We're both sticking around. It makes sense that we be together."

Although Truman still looked skeptical, Dawson appeared to be considering his words. "Two of the SWAT personnel in one place? They'd smell a trap for sure."

Dace folded his arms over his chest. "If they bother to do research, they'll discover Jolie and I…have a history. That would make our living arrangements seem more reasonable. If they don't…" He lifted a shoulder. "No offense, but these guys have managed to outsmart the FBI on a dozen different bank heists. Even if they smell a trap, why wouldn't they believe they can outmaneuver you again?"

"Listen, Recker…" Truman took a step toward him.

Dawson put up a hand to halt the other agent. "You could be right. Give me a chance to run this by SAC Fenholt. And Chief Sanders," he added as an afterthought.

"We're not going to sit around doing nothing." Dace had already given it some thought. There's no way he and Jolie could be in the same place together for days on end with nothing to distract them. "If we're going to have a security detail on us, we won't be on active duty. Tell Fenholt she may as well use us on the task force."

"That will be up to SAC Fenholt," Dawson said noncommittally.

"It's a condition of our involvement," Dace corrected, "and it's nonnegotiable. I can't believe you have so much manpower you can afford to turn down the offer."

Truman shuffled his feet. "For two people claiming to want to help, you have lots of conditions. Do you have a mommy we need to be concerned about, too?"

Too? "No." Dace let the sarcasm roll off him, but the words struck a chord. His mother was safely out of town visiting his sister in Tucson, but she was due back next

Tuesday. He'd have to come up with a plausible reason for keeping her in Arizona for a couple more weeks without giving her enough information that would have her racing home to check on him. It would be a balancing act, but he'd figure something out.

The door to Jolie's room swung open and the doctor stepped out, a look of frustration on his creased face. "That is one very stubborn lady. I'd like to keep her another day for observation. Maybe one of you can convince her."

The feds looked at Dace. He could have told them they were wasting their time. There had been only one time when he'd had any luck convincing Jolie of anything, and that had ended in tragedy. He didn't have that kind of power anymore. And he no longer wanted the responsibility for it.

"She's going to do what she wants," he said finally. The doctor threw up his hands and walked away, muttering something about the lack of intelligence in law enforcement in general. Dawson slipped his hand in the pocket of his immaculate suit trousers and considered him. Uncomfortable, Dace lifted a shoulder. "The sooner we can get this operation underway, the faster we can draw this guy out. And if you haven't figured it out by now, you're wasting your breath trying to talk Jolie out of leaving."

There was a melodic ringing and Dawson took a pager out of the pocket of his jacket. Checking the display, he said, "It's SAC Fenholt. I have to update her on all this." Seeming to make a decision, he looked at Dace. "Both of you need to stay put long enough for us to get a detail in place. Then your home will have to be thoroughly checked out. Once we're done, whoever gets assigned to your security will accompany you there. Don't leave the hospital before the agent arrives."

With a slight inclination of his head, Dace agreed. The man switched his attention to Truman. "You can head over to

Conrad's apartment and check on her mother. Stick close until we decide on a safe house to stash her in for the meantime."

The man's words made no sense. "I don't know where you guys got your information, but there's no one else living at Jolie's place. She doesn't have a mother." She'd been close-mouthed about her childhood but she'd been clear about that. Her parents were dead. She'd been raised by her grandmother. She'd told him that much, and since the memories didn't seem to be happy ones, he hadn't pressed. He had often wondered if her status as an orphan accounted for her inability to believe in a family. In her doubting the appearance of anything, anyone good in her life.

Truman gave him a sour grin, clearly not happy with his assignment. "Guess you don't know as much about Conrad as you thought, Recker. But then, maybe you didn't spend much time talking when you two were…making that history."

The agent turned on his heel and walked swiftly away so Dace swung his gaze to Dawson, who was regarding him quizzically. "I'm not sure what the confusion is, but Conrad specifically told us that security for her mother was a condition of her involvement. You must have misunderstood."

There was a buzzing in his ears. A clenching in his gut. "Yeah." He gave a grim smile. "That must be it." The agent walked away, leaving Dace feeling as if he'd taken a hammer in the chest.

He'd misunderstood all right. She'd lied to him, even after they'd gotten closer. After they'd lived together, had a child together, she'd kept right on lying.

She had a mother. The knowledge was a drumbeat in his skull. And the woman lived right here in Metro City.

Had she known about Sammy? Had the woman even been at the funeral? He searched his memory. The day had been a blur but it had been a private service, with only friends and family.

There'd been no family there for her. Just like there had been none at the hospital when Sammy had been born. There had been plenty of Dace's relatives, enough to fairly suffocate a loner like Jolie. After his mother and three sisters swooped in, he'd recognized the faint panic on Jolie's face and tried to run interference for her. He'd thought he'd understood the source of the no-trespassing signs clearly marked around the mother of his son. Thought he'd recognized what had turned her into the guarded woman he'd once shared a life with.

The joke was on him. Turned out he hadn't known her at all.

At the faint sound of the door pushing open again, Jolie shoved her arms in the sleeves of her shirt, glancing over her shoulder, faintly annoyed. This room had all the privacy of a fishbowl. But if it was a nurse coming with those papers for her to sign, releasing her despite doctor's orders, it would be a welcome interruption.

Instead, Dace stood in the doorway. "Don't bother knocking," she said caustically. "No one else does." She fastened the garment, finding the bottom two buttons missing. The shirt showed more than a little wear, with a rip nearly halfway up one side, and a stain smeared across the front.

Blood. Hers. She sucked in a breath and bent carefully to the bag someone had placed all her garments in to retrieve her shoes and socks. She'd learned earlier that bending over too fast brought on a wave of dizziness that nearly toppled her. She didn't think it was wise to show that weakness in front of Dace.

"I heard the doctor out there. If you're here to convince me to stay another night, save yourself some time."

He didn't answer, just lounged against the door, his gaze never leaving her. She sat down, more than a little glad to have an excuse, and propped one ankle over her knee to aid in finishing dressing, moving cautiously. Her pants were ripped, the hole corresponding with a sutured gash on her thigh. The wound throbbed every time she moved.

Dace wasn't wearing the same clothes he'd had on yesterday, so somewhere along the line he'd gone home, or someone had dropped fresh clothes off for him. But not a razor. Whiskers a shade darker than his close-cropped chestnut hair shadowed his face. She recognized the faded jeans as his favorites, worn white in the most interesting places. One booted foot was crossed over the other. He looked hard. Unyielding. And more than a little mean.

She slipped one sock on and bent slowly to snag the shoe. "So." Something in his silence was making her uneasy. "The feds go to arrange things?"

"Yeah."

He still hadn't moved, and being fixed by that intense unswerving stare was worsening a headache already approaching migraine status. "We need to talk about what you said earlier. About staying, too. You've got to realize it's unnecessary. We've got nothing to gain with two of us sticking around, instead of just one." She had to uncross her leg to shove her foot into the shoe, and even that small jolt had her skull weeping. Gritting her teeth, she started on the other foot.

"You've got Della to think about, too," she continued. Della was his mother, a friendly open woman who doted on her family. She'd doted on Sammy, those few months. Although Jolie had recognized the reservations Della might have had regarding her and their arrangement, she'd never doubted the woman's feelings for her grandson.

Dace still said nothing.

"You could take her to one of your sisters. Visit the family for a while until this whole thing is over."

"I could."

He moved his shoulders in a not-quite shrug. She was distracted for a moment by the action. Had they always been that broad? That thick? There had been a time when she'd explored every inch of his body, touching, tasting at will. A time when she'd known it better than any other man's.

To avoid the unbidden memories that chose that moment to appear, she stood, stamping her shoe on and the mental images out. He was just a man. Not so different from any man she'd slept with. More annoying than some. Certainly more stubborn. Circumstances had led them down a path she'd never envisioned for herself but she'd learned the hard way the folly of reaching for something that wasn't meant to be. Not for her.

"Of course, I could argue that you could send *your* mother out of harm's way, too." A fissure of ice trickled down her spine, freezing her from the inside out. Sudden dreadful comprehension followed. Of course the agents had mentioned something about Trixie. And he would think… It was all too easy to figure out what he thought. It was there in his expression, in the twist of his lips, the derision in his eyes.

She reached for something to say, came up with nothing. *Lies always catch up with liars.* That little profundity was courtesy of Lila Porter, foster mother number three. What she'd lacked in warmth she'd made up for with such thought-provoking insights. Another of her favorites had been *blood will tell.* Jolie had spent much of her life hoping that wasn't true. Fearing it was.

"Nothing to say?" Dace's voice was caustic. "I'd like to hear about the mother-daughter reunion after her resurrection. Must have been quite touching. Does she know about her untimely demise?"

With her hand on the back of the chair to steady herself, Jolie stood, swaying only slightly. "Knock it off, Dace."

He slapped his palm sharply against the door in back of him. The crack of sound speared through the hammering in her head. "Why'd you bother lying about her? To me? Because if I know one thing about you, Jolie, it's that you were closer to me than you let yourself get to anyone else in a long, long time."

She opened her mouth to answer, but whatever she was about to say was cut short with an abrupt gesture of his hand. "No. Don't deny it. You know it's true."

Of course she knew it was true. And that was what had made their relationship so unlikely. So terrifying. "You wouldn't understand."

He gave a curt nod, his eyes still lethal. "Maybe not. But you made that decision for me, didn't you? Seems like you were making lots of decisions for me back then."

"Don't." Her voice was sharp. "Don't make this about two years ago. Don't rehash things that are only going hurt both of us. What does it matter now? She wasn't in my life. Now she is. There isn't any more to it than that."

His expression eased slightly, but she didn't fool herself into thinking his temper had been defused. "Wrong. There's always more to it. You dole out pieces of yourself pretty damn sparingly, Jolie. You decide what personal details to share or whether to share them at all. You're a freakin' emotional Fort Knox."

The accusation surprised a bitter laugh from her. "Please. I'm a realist. We come from two totally different places. I knew that, even if you didn't. Your mother is June Cleaver, okay? Mine is…not. She wasn't relevant when we were together. But now she's back and she's terminally ill. She doesn't have a damn thing to do with you and me. She never did."

But even as she uttered the words, she tasted the lie. Regardless of how little time she'd spent with Trixie, their relationship had inevitably shaped the woman she'd become. And knowing that, accepting it, had influenced every aspect of Jolie's life.

Even she realized that that was a pretty big impact for a woman who'd been absent during most of her formative years.

"You're right about one thing." Dace shoved away from the door, jamming his hands in his jeans pockets. "It doesn't matter anymore. You and I were over a long time ago. What we need to concentrate on now is staying alive. Given the feds' handling of this case so far, I have my doubts about our chances."

She didn't answer because she was having doubts, too. Not of their survival. She lacked Dace's pessimism there. But she did question how they were going to get through this thing when they were all but attached at the hip for the duration.

Metro City Police Chief Carl Sanders sat at the conference table, his piercing gaze trained on Jolie. It was all she could do not to squirm under the assessing look. "You look like hell, Conrad. You sure you're up for this?"

"Yes, sir. I am." She still hadn't gotten a chance to change her clothes, and no doubt her appearance didn't inspire confidence. Her headache had subsided to a constant dull throb that left her feeling perpetually muzzy. But she imbued her voice with as much strength as she could muster.

Her words didn't appear to reassure him. He looked at Dace. "I'm not crazy about using two of my detectives as bait. Hell, I'm not crazy about using one. But near as I can see, you're just icing on the cake, Recker. The rest of your squad has no problem lying low for a while. Seems like a good idea for you to do the same."

His voice was respectful, but as implacable as the chief's. "I'm in, sir. It makes sense for the two of us to do this together."

Sanders gave him a hard look, but said only, "All right then. I assume you both know the chance you're taking."

"Yes, sir. We're ready to go ahead with this."

Jolie's response just made the man's expression even grimmer. Sanders looked across the table. The chairs were lined with FBI personnel, many of whom Jolie hadn't met before. "Well, Special Agent in Charge Fenholt, let's hear what you have so far. I'm not allowing you to use my detectives for tiger bait unless I can be damn sure it's a necessity. And that they'll be protected."

Fenholt sat directly across from the chief. She pushed an accordion file over to Sanders, who extracted the contents and began looking through them. "We were able to get enough DNA from the blood the HT left at the bank to run tests," she began. "Once we have the results we'll be able to cross-check with CODIS and the state criminal DNA database. We're coordinating closely with our antiterrorism unit, and they'll facilitate running the DNA through the Department of Homeland Security's database on international terrorists."

That news had Jolie's attention snapping to the woman. A quick glance around the table showed similar reactions from all the locals.

Fenholt seemed to choose her words carefully. "About two months ago a confidential informant gave us what we believe to be solid intelligence regarding a terrorist sleeper cell operating here in California. Without going into detail, DHS verified the existence of the cell, believed to be operated by American-born al Qaeda sympathizers. We're pursuing the possibility that they're hitting banks to fund a future strike somewhere on the West Coast."

Stunned, Jolie could only look at the expressions of the federal agents. This thing had more far-reaching implications than she'd first believed. The possible targets in the area were endless. And devastating.

"I'm telling you this only so you'll understand what's at stake." Fenholt wore a grim mask. "If there's even the slightest chance of drawing these people out, we're going to take it."

She slanted a look at Dawson, who took up where she left off. "We've successfully moved Detective Conrad's mother to a safe house and one of our agents will stay with her at all times." He shifted his attention to Jolie and Dace. "We've gone through your place thoroughly and it's secure. An agent will be stationed with you at all times, and a car and driver will be provided. For any public appearances, of course, you'll have a full tactical team covering you."

She and Dace exchanged a look. Sanders raised his head sharply. "Public appearances?"

Fenholt took over. "If the HT's accomplices are still in the area, they may try for the detectives where they appear the most vulnerable, in their home. We can prepare for that. Or we can be more daring and plan something that is sure to draw the accomplices out, if they're still around."

Sanders was no fool. "I assume you already have something in mind."

"The last of the funerals for the agent and officers who were killed last week will be held tomorrow." Fenholt's jaw tightened. "It would seem reasonable to hold a public memorial for them on Saturday."

"Let me guess." Sanders's voice was steely. "Recker and Conrad would be on prominent display."

A trickle of unease made its way down Jolie's spine. The bank robbery was still fodder for the nightly news. The memorial would be a public spectacle, full of media, politicians and rubberneckers, as well as law enforcement and their families. An event that large would be a security nightmare.

Guilt stabbed her. She'd signed on for this. But Dace would be exposed, too, in a way he'd probably never considered when he'd elbowed his way in. Not for the first time, she cursed that stubborn protective streak of his that had him believing he always needed to ride to the rescue. She would have thought their past would have eliminated his Galahad quality, at least where she was concerned.

Sanders exchanged a quick glance with his deputy chief, clearly unconvinced. "Why don't you just paint targets on their foreheads and be done with it?"

"We've given this a lot of thought. With national media coverage prior, I think the service will be an irresistible temptation to the accomplices, wherever they may be. We'll have full tactical and sniper response in place, and the site will receive the highest level of security," Fenholt assured him.

"Until something goes wrong." He shook his head. "Not good enough. We'll go ahead and plan the memorial. But my department will provide additional security."

The special agent fingered the bifocals hanging from a chain around her neck. "You're talking a lot of man-hours."

"It's the only way my detectives will take part." Sanders's voice was adamant. "Take it or leave it."

After a slight hesitation, Fenholt nodded. "We'll coordinate the details with your office." The matter resolved, she shifted her attention to Jolie and the silent man beside her. "Special Agent Dawson passed along your willingness to participate in the investigation. We appreciate the interagency cooperation. We can always use a couple extra pair of hands, at least for the duration of this case." It was painfully clear to Jolie that the SAC's words were for Sanders's benefit. It remained to be seen just how deeply she and Dace would be allowed to delve into the task force intelligence.

But their participation would provide a welcome diversion. With Dace at her side, she was certain to need one.

By the time Jolie followed Dace and Agent Hart up the walk to the town house they'd be staying in, her body nearly wept in gratitude. Not for anything would she have admitted just how good a bed sounded right now. It had gotten increasingly difficult to concentrate as the meeting had stretched into the late hours. Her brain felt as though it were stuffed with cotton.

Fenholt had explained that there would be two agents stationed outside, while Dawson and Truman would take turns providing interior protection. Agent Hart had drawn Trixie detail, a task she was certain would prove one of the most challenging of the young man's career. Dawson had provided her with Hart's cell-phone number. It was too late now, but she'd call Trixie tomorrow morning and try to gauge the woman's understanding of the turn of events.

She frowned when Dace stepped forward to unlock the door. What was he doing with the key to the safe house?

"Detective Conrad?"

Dawson's questioning tone came from behind her shoulder. Still grappling with her confusion, she followed Dace over the threshold. Watched him slip the keys into his pocket and cross to the answering machine on the counter. Play back the messages. She froze, comprehension belatedly slamming into her.

They weren't going to be staying in some anonymous FBI safe house. This was Dace's home.

Dawson brushed by her and slipped out of his suit jacket, hung it over the back of a chair pushed up to the center island in the kitchen. Maybe she'd underestimated the damage done to her head in the explosion. She wasn't usually dense, but this little detail had skated right by her.

"You'll have to take the couch, Dawson. But I can round up sheets and a pillow." Dace indicated a door across the room. "There's a bathroom through there. Jolie and I will use the one upstairs."

The agent worked his shoulders tiredly. "That sounds great right now. And under the circumstances, you can call me Anthony."

Dace nodded, looked at Jolie. "The second bedroom is outfitted as an office. There's a foldout couch in it, though, that's supposed to be halfway comfortable. I told the agents to put your stuff in there."

He turned to lead the way and Jolie fell in behind him, weariness making it difficult to walk without stumbling. She'd given a list to Dawson of the things she needed from her apartment. She supposed it was too late to be worrying about someone pawing around in her personals, but still, the thought made her sort of…

She stopped in her tracks, her heart leaping to her throat, staring at the mantel above a fireplace that probably never got used. It was crowded with framed pictures. Of Dace with his mother, his sisters. Of him standing, grinning like a fiend, with nieces and nephews wrapped around him like limpets.

But it was the photos in the center of the bunch that had her heart clutching, the oxygen leaching from her lungs.

Chapter 7

Sammy.

Jolie felt herself sway. The photos were like a visual banquet for a woman who'd starved herself too long. She took an involuntary step toward the pictures, her gaze sweeping over them hungrily.

With a kick in her chest, she recognized the one of her son only minutes old, naked and wrinkled, being held up to Dace's shoulder. And the one they'd snapped of his first baby grin, his mouth wide and toothless. Her throat closed at the sight.

When she'd left Metro City, she'd wanted only to escape the memories that brought the slashing pain. She'd left everything behind that would remind her of the loss she was fleeing. She'd told herself that was the safest thing. The smartest.

She'd regretted it almost every day since.

Dace hadn't run from the memories. Instead he'd put them on display, and she greedily devoured them, even as she wondered how he could bear to see them every day. To remember.

But in a flash she recognized her mistake. Not having any photos of Sammy hadn't stemmed her memories. It had only made the specifics of her son's appearance go fuzzy around the edges, while the pain had remained undulled.

Dace was coming back down the steps from the second level with an armful of sheets and a pillow. She looked up then, caught his gaze on her. There was a softness there that nearly undid her, blended with an understanding only he could share. And it was all too easy to recall exactly what had drawn her to him in the first place. What had persuaded her to throw her well-honed caution to the winds. And what had kept her at his side, long after the life had sputtered from their relationship.

He continued past her, dropped the pillow and sheets on the couch. When he turned, she forced herself to move, nearly stumbling with the effort. She followed him up six steps to the second level of the condominium.

"The bathroom is at the end of the hall. Your room is here." He reached inside the first door on their right and flicked on the light. "Sheets, blankets and pillows are in the closet." When she remained unmoving, he brushed by her, opened the closet door to show her the bedding stacked neatly on the shelves at one side.

Jolie flicked a glance over the space. Her suitcases were piled next to an overstuffed navy couch. The room was neat, impersonal, as if he spent little time in here. Dace had always had a habit of leaving his belongings strewn around, although he'd always cleaned up after himself eventually.

The rolltop desk in the corner had the lid closed, and she'd be willing to bet if it were raised she'd find its top littered with bills and correspondence, the contents in no particular order. At one time the lack of organization had driven her nuts, even as she realized that her need for order sprang from a childhood absent of it.

There were more framed pictures on top of the desk. Most featured Dace with buddies of his from the force. But there was also one of Sammy in his infant swing. Another showed Della holding him, their faces close together.

In two swift strides Dace crossed to the desk, picked up the pictures. "I can put them away while you're here."

She shook her head. "You don't have to." Seeing photos of Sammy after all this time had a different effect on her than she'd expected. The sight of him hurt, but it also filled a part of her that had gone cold and dark since she'd left.

Without a conscious decision, she closed the distance between them, took the framed pictures out of his hands and looked down at them. "I didn't take any when I left."

"I know."

Her eyes burning, she continued, "But it wasn't because I was trying to forget him. It just…it all hurt so much. I just wanted to leave the pain behind."

Dace's voice was quiet. "I know that, too. I guess I always did."

He reached out and touched her then, one crooked finger sliding lightly along her jaw, and her eyes closed against the wash of sensation trailing in its wake. There had been too many hits in the past twenty-four hours, one piling on top of the other until her defenses were not just weakened but lying in a shambles. She needed time to regroup. She knew that. But acting on the realization seemed beyond her.

His lips brushed hers, whisper soft, and a sob she'd never release knotted in her chest. There was danger here. She could recognize that even as she accepted the outcome. His taste was familiar and so was the yearning it elicited. That longing had always alarmed her. A man who could make her *want,* in any way but the physical, was a threat to the control she'd spent a lifetime building.

His tongue traced the seam of her lips and they parted of their own accord. Her breath caught. It would be easy to deny the heat that had always flared to life between them. All too easy to recall where it led. But this tenderness from him was devastating to senses already shredded by the events of the day.

He touched her nowhere else. There was only the soft pressure of mouth against mouth, the connection as light as gossamer. Her fingers clutched around the frames she still held, needing something substantial to hold on to. Afraid that without it, she'd reach for him.

Somehow their entire past seemed tied up in the kiss. Everything that had gone before. The passion. The joy. The sorrow. The regrets. As her lips moved beneath his she wondered what it said about their future.

As if in response to that thought, the tenuous connection was broken. Her eyes flickered open in delayed reaction just in time to see him walking out the door. He didn't look back.

Taking a shaky breath, Jolie acknowledged that he had the right idea. They couldn't afford to look back. The past held nothing but heartache. And with someone out there trying to kill them, they were going to have their hands full dealing with the present.

"This is crap." Dace tossed down his pen in frustration. "Interagency cooperation, my ass. We're nothing but glorified paper shufflers."

Jolie looked up from the sheaf of papers she was reading. They were the only occupants of the small windowless conference room. After a great deal of debate, Sanders and Fenholt had decided it would look most natural to have them working at the police administration building. If the subject was watching their movements, they could ill afford to be followed to the temporary offices the FBI was using.

Which meant they had limited access to the case files the feds had compiled so far—only what they needed to follow up on whatever lead the force determined. Given the first few hours of their assignment, she had to agree with Dace's assessment.

"At least you have Sanders's copy of the case file," she said, swallowing a yawn. The chief, familiar with the Bureau's idea of information sharing, had done what he could to provide them with the tools they'd need to actually contribute to the investigation. Besides giving them the case file this morning, he'd outfitted the room with two laptops with high-speed Internet access and a printer. "My eyes are ready to start bleeding. Some of these bank robbery records go back to the sixties. The ex-cons are collecting social security by now."

It was their first day on the job since she'd left the hospital. Yesterday had been spent replacing her cell phone, driver's license and credit cards, and both of them had had insurance companies to deal with on their cars. Then each of them had mothers to contact.

She'd overheard Dace speaking with Della. He'd concocted a creative story about pipes bursting and making a mess of her kitchen. He was an admirable liar. He'd managed to convince his mother to stay in Arizona for a couple weeks while he handled the cleanup.

Her call to Trixie hadn't gone quite as smoothly. The woman had rejected Jolie's explanation regarding the precautionary move, and had been even more verbal about her dislike of Agent Hart. On that measure, at least, Jolie could sympathize. She'd ended the conversation by talking to Hart herself and arranging for him to bring Trixie to meet Jolie at a restaurant that evening for dinner. It was doubtful her mother would be any more reasonable in person. She had several more hours to come up with an excuse to leave Dace behind. She was less willing than ever to have the two of them meet.

Dace rolled his chair back from the table and stretched before rising in one lithe movement and sauntering over to her. Instantly, her muscles tensed. With everything else going on yesterday, it had been easy to shove aside the memory of that ill-advised kiss.

Her pulse began to thud, slow and heavy. Emotions had been close to the surface. They'd both experienced shocks that would have laid some people flat. *Had* laid her flat, at least overnight. And then being hit with those photos of Sammy had rocked her even more.

The excuses came quickly, but rang false. So she hadn't been at the top of her game the night before. It was just as true that no one could sneak under her guard like Dace Recker. She'd known that, yet still hadn't avoided a kiss that had summoned all-too-dangerous memories. The two of them had been combustible, once upon a time. It would be a mistake to recall that portion of their past without also re-membering the pain of how they'd ended.

Nothing could ever convince her to willingly go through that agony again. And based on Dace's distant behavior since the kiss, he must agree.

He propped his hands on the table next to her to peer at her notes. "Making lists. That's a first." He managed, barely, to dodge the elbow she sent to his ribs. She was meticulous in her note-taking. So sue her.

He studied the chart she'd been working on. She'd started with the most recent of the files they'd been given, those dating in the early nineties. She'd noted felons who'd been convicted of bank robbery in the state of California or surrounding states. Since the crime was usually a younger person's choice, she'd cut off the ages at fifty and excluded any felons who were still incarcerated or dead. It was a depressingly long list.

"The feds are going to pursue the strongest leads," he said finally. "That's why we're left tracking down the long shots."

His prediction was depressing but most likely true. "I overheard Dawson talking about the security tapes. I'm sure they're comparing the surveillance footage to that in the other robberies."

Dace straightened. "And cross-checking for glimpses of the hostage taker or his accomplices prior to the robbery attempt. Someone had to scout the location. Plant the explosive devices."

Jolie dropped her pen, leaned back in her chair. "Maybe we're overlooking the obvious. This guy is something of an anomaly because we can be positive he wasn't working alone. Eighty percent of bank robbers are solitary offenders."

"And he's smart," Dace put in grimly. He propped his hips on the table next to her, crossed his arms over his chest. "Takes the time for subtle disguises. Does his homework beforehand. Most guys go to knock over a bank, they'll choose the end of the week, midday, when the bank is full of customers."

"Shows he's a professional," Jolie agreed. "Monday morning he's hoping for the weekend deposits to up his take. Earlier in the day means fewer customers, a crime scene that's easier to control. Dawson said he always filled the bag himself, so he knows enough to avoid the die packs a fast-thinking teller would put in a cash bag."

"From the surveillance footage Fenholt showed us, the HT looked too young to have done time for a previous robbery."

Nodding, she picked up the list she'd been working on. "But maybe someone he knew was in the system. Father, uncle, brother…he had someone in his life he was close to. That much was clear from the conversations we had."

Dace frowned, considering. "You think he was talking about his accomplice in the bank heists?"

"It's possible. Any of these guys sent away in the early nineties could be out by now. The robberies started six months ago. What if we focus on the ones released in the past twenty-four months and see what we come up with?"

He lifted a shoulder, clearly not excited at the prospect, but Jolie was already picking up her pen, ready to pore through the notes she'd taken.

"What do you suggest we do once we get the list narrowed down?" Dace jerked his head to the closed door. Their FBI protection was outside it. "Take our watchdog with us as we go hunt the guy down?"

Not put off by his less-than-eager response, she started circling names that fit the parameters of their search. "No. I'd suggest you use the department computer over there and contact prisons where these guys did their time. See if you can get copies of their visitor lists. Oh, and it wouldn't hurt to get the names of their cell mates, while you're at it."

She could sense his gaze on her but refused to look up. His task would put him on the far side of the room, and she was honest enough to admit that she'd welcome the distance.

"All right," he said finally. He held out his hand and she handed him the first sheet of names she'd underlined. "Guess you're calling the shots."

There was something more than a bit caustic in his tone that made her think he wasn't referring only to the present.

She knew better than to respond. If she was calling the shots, their relationship would stay on this exact footing. Strictly professional with no hint of personal involvement.

Because when this was over, she had no doubts that they'd both walk away without a backward glance. Neither of them was in any hurry to make the same mistake all over again.

Jolie entered the restaurant ahead of Agent Michael Hawkins, the fed assigned as their driver and chief watchdog away from the apartment. Scanning the interior, she quickly saw Agent Hart and Trixie near the back. They appeared to be arguing, and she stifled a sigh. Maybe the agency would recommend the man for a commendation after this assignment. Certainly he'd have earned it after putting up with Trixie's theatrics for the duration.

"Detective Conrad." Hart rose lazily to his feet as Jolie approached their booth. He looked over her shoulder, past Hawkins. "Where's Recker?"

"He and Dawson stayed behind to discuss the case." And it had taken some fast-talking to make that happen. She'd told Dace that it would be helpful if he could pick Dawson's brain regarding the course of the investigation. And though he likely saw through her attempt to leave him behind, he hadn't objected. He'd only warned her to stick close to Hawkins.

She'd left, relieved. Dace had emotionally backpedaled since that first devastating loss of control, and his distance helped her maintain her own. They could do this. They'd take part in the investigation, as much as the feds would allow. See this thing through. And then they'd go their separate ways. Metro City had a half-million people. Surely she and Dace could coexist within its confines without causing each other too much trouble.

"Trixie." She summoned a smile for her mother and slid

into the booth across from her. Flicking a glance toward the agent, she said politely, "I hope she hasn't been giving you any trouble."

Hart stood. "The day I can't handle a babysitting detail is the day I'll hand in my badge. Hawkins and I will sit at the table over there." He jerked his head to indicate an empty table for two kitty-corner from the booth. "Give you two some privacy."

She gave a short nod, and the two men moved away. Shifting her attention to her mother, she did a quick survey. Although Trixie didn't look the worse for wear, there was a peevish cast to her expression that didn't bode well for the evening.

Jolie picked up a menu. "Have you ordered yet? I'm starved."

"How much longer do I got to have that guy hanging over my shoulder?" Trixie demanded. "He's like a damn ghost the way he's always lurking 'round. I can barely take a leak without him following me into the can."

Since her mother had made no effort to keep her voice down, there was no doubt that Hart overheard her. As did every occupant in the restaurant within twenty feet. "Lower your voice." The layer of steel in Jolie's tone made it an order, rather than a request. "You and I can have a discussion without everyone in the restaurant listening in."

Trixie shot her a glare but her next words were a subdued whine. "Least you'd go to work most days and give me some alone time. I need my space, y'know? That guy gives me claustrophobia, he sticks so close."

"That's his job. The explosion outside my apartment complex was meant for me." She'd explained this to the woman over the phone once already. "If the subject knows where I live, it follows he could still strike out at you even if

I'm not there anymore. This is for your own protection until he's caught."

"I can take care of myself." The door of the restaurant opened and the woman flicked a glance at the newcomers. "I've been on my own since I was fifteen. Didn't need no one watching over me and telling me what to do then. Still don't."

There was truth in her words. At fifteen, Trixie had run away. She'd been doing exactly as she pleased ever since.

"It won't be for long." Neither the department nor the Bureau had unlimited resources. Their efforts would have to garner results soon, or the investigation would be turned in a different direction. Financial considerations were a daily reality of law enforcement work.

"They have some Southwestern dishes." Determinedly, Jolie shifted topics. "Are you still in the mood for Mexican?"

Trixie lifted her bony shoulders, bare above the red tube top she wore with her black painted-on capris. "Don't have much appetite these days with the kiddie fed hanging over my shoulder every minute." She raised her voice a little. "Never liked cops. Haven't changed my mind the past couple days."

And it wouldn't occur to the woman that Jolie was included in that assessment, as well. Even if it had, she doubted it would alter Trixie's opinion. Knowing that didn't bother her. There had never been any pretense between them. Trixie had never bothered to act like she gave a damn. Jolie didn't have to pretend tender feelings for the woman who'd borne her. There were no surprises when each knew exactly where the other stood.

A waitress appeared next to the booth, wearing a crisp pink uniform and a fixed smile. "What can I get you girls today? Do you want to hear about our specials?"

"I'll have a cheeseburger, plain, with fries and coffee."

Jolie closed the plastic-coated menu and slipped it back into its holder. "Trixie? Are you getting anything?"

"May as well get a bite." The other woman sent a lingering glance toward the front door of the place before returning her gaze to the menu. "Not really hungry, but I suppose you'll rat me out to Baxter if I don't eat something." Despite her words, she rattled off an order that would feed a very hungry truck driver on a cross-country run.

The waitress moved away and stopped by the agents' table. Jolie watched as the two men halted their conversation to order. Hawkins looked to be about Hart's age, but the similarities stopped there. So far she'd found Hawkins to be quiet, but helpful and friendly. He lacked the other man's cocky manner.

When she looked back at Trixie, she again found her watching the front door. Jolie followed the direction of her gaze and saw a lone man approaching a stool at the counter. "Are you expecting someone?"

"Just people watching." The other woman returned her attention to Jolie, her eyes narrowed. "Haven't been getting out much," she said pointedly.

And apparently that was cramping Trixie's style. Despite herself, amusement bloomed. Jolie kept as tight a rein on her as she could, but as Trixie had mentioned, she was at work much of the time. And her SWAT rotation called for after-hours training every third day. If this assignment could have any unexpected benefits, having Trixie under round-the-clock surveillance was one.

"Hear you're living with your old boyfriend. Recker."

Humor was replaced with wariness, even while something inside her reared away from the word. *Boyfriend.* Whatever Dace had once meant to her, the word sounded foreign. Jolie reached for her water glass. "Where'd you hear that?"

"I ain't stupid." Trixie jerked her chin toward Hart. "Overheard him on the phone, that you were at Recker's place. Hope you aren't thinking about dancing to that tune again."

Since Jolie had never mentioned Dace's name to Trixie, it was obvious the woman had overheard more than she'd let on. "We're working a job together, and there's a federal agent staying there, too. I'm hardly 'living' with him." Movements careful, Jolie set the glass down again. The last person she wanted to discuss Dace with was Trixie.

"Like I said, I ain't stupid." Trixie lit another cigarette, let her gaze wander around the interior of the restaurant. "Had more than my share of men trailing after me over the years. I know what's what. You got my looks. Men are gonna hang around you, too. Just be smarter this time. Don't let him knock you up again."

There was a vise in her chest, squeezing the breath from her lungs. It took a moment to manage speech. "A little late to be dispensing maternal advice, isn't it?"

The sarcasm was wasted on Trixie. "We're not much alike, you and me." She tilted her head back, blew a perfect smoke ring. "But we're the same in one way. Neither of us was meant to be mothers. Don't make us bad people. Just makes us realistic." Abruptly, she lowered her hand to stub out her cigarette. "I gotta pee."

She slid out of the booth and reached for her oversize bag, hitching it over one shoulder before sauntering away, an exaggerated swing to her skinny hips. And Jolie was left to deal with the quick verbal jabs she'd landed before leaving.

Trixie's words carved a hollow through her center, filling the void with ice. She knew better than to listen to them. The woman was merely projecting her flaws onto Jolie. She didn't know her daughter. How could she? Jolie hadn't spent any significant time with her mother since the age of five. Trixie was hardly in the position to render a character analysis.

And yet…hadn't she told herself exactly the same thing, over and over in the past year and a half? She'd known nothing about mothers. Nothing about acting like one. Nothing about being one. She'd recognized that fact from the first. It was why Dace had had to work so hard the moment she'd told him of the pregnancy.

With trembling hands, she reached for her water glass and took a sip.

She almost hadn't told Dace at all. They'd been together less than three months. After the first positive test result, she'd bought two more home pregnancy kits, sure that there had been a mistake. But the stick had turned blue, not once, but three times.

There'd been a mistake, all right. Forgetting that the Pill was only ninety-nine percent effective had been hers.

She'd lined up an appointment for an abortion before it had even occurred to her to tell Dace. And she wasn't particularly proud of that fact. Belatedly the realization had struck her that if she withheld that information from him, she was no better than Trixie had been, all those years ago.

Recognition of that fact had been enough for her to swallow her fears, and her pride, and give him a chance to agree with her. Of course an abortion was the best option. The logical choice. They'd make the decision together. They'd been a couple. That's what couples did.

But Dace hadn't agreed.

I know it's supposed to be a woman's decision. The hell with that. It's our *decision, Jolie. Yours and mine. Let's not think about what would be easiest. Let's think about what could be. We could be a family. You just have to give us a chance.*

It'd taken him weeks, but he'd worn her down. She shook her head numbly. Useless to wonder how he'd shattered defenses a lifetime in the making. Dace Recker was a bulldozer when he wanted something, and as a negotiator he'd been well versed in the art of persuasion.

And if she were honest she'd admit that Dace could undermine her guard the way no one else had ever managed. He'd hit on the one thing she'd long ago stopped hoping for. A family.

"Where's your mother?"

Jolie's head jerked at Hart's question. She glanced over at the agents' table. "Bathroom." How long had the woman been gone? She looked toward the back, where the restrooms were housed, then did a quick scan of the room. But her mind wasn't really on what she saw.

Trixie's voice resonated in her mind. *Neither of us was meant to be mothers.* The words only wounded because Jolie had feared the same thing all along.

Something nagged at her, finally making its way through her misery. She looked around at the occupants more carefully, lingering at the empty stool at the counter. A moment later the man she'd seen sitting there made his way from the back. But he bypassed the place he'd sat. Left the cup of coffee he'd ordered and headed out the front door.

Jolie slid out of the booth and strode rapidly to the restroom. Suspicion bloomed quickly where Trixie was concerned. And in most cases it was warranted.

She pushed open the door, saw no one standing at the sinks. But a quick glance pinpointed Trixie's location. Her brightly colored handbag was on the floor near the closed door of the stall. Without a word, Jolie crossed to the door and reached beneath it, snagging the bag.

"What the hell? You picked the wrong woman to steal from, bitch!" The stall door was flung open and Trixie hurtled from the opening, nearly stopping in mid-motion when she saw Jolie emptying her bag onto the vanity counter.

Lipsticks. Three of them. A set of keys, maybe to her old apartment.

"Gimme that!" Trixie screeched, making a grab for the purse.

Jolie easily deflected the movement, continuing her inventory. Crumpled receipts, yellowed with age. A list of phone numbers. A billfold with—surprisingly—fifty dollars in it. A wallet. Flipping it open, she was not surprised to see Agent Hart's unsmiling visage staring back at her from the ID. And finally—what she'd been dreading, but expecting. A small clear baggie filled with white crystals. Enough to keep Trixie in a drug-induced haze for the next forty-eight hours.

"That's mine!" The older woman launched herself at Jolie, grabbing at the arm holding the baggie aloft. Her grip was amazingly strong, the invectives that spewed from her mouth amazingly imaginative. "You got no right to take my stuff. I paid for that!"

"I suspect that Agent Hart paid for it. Indirectly." Jolie dodged the fist Trixie swung at her, but didn't manage to evade the kick sent to her leg. Her sutured wound screamed at the impact.

"You think you can take over my life? Who asked you? Who wanted you?" The woman screamed the words as she struck out wildly, biting, hitting, kicking. "I don't need no one telling me what to do. I don't need you! Too bad that bomb didn't blow you to hell and back!"

"Yeah, too bad." Unable to subdue the woman any other way, Jolie finally wrapped her arms around her in an unbreakable restraint. Trixie's wild struggles didn't lessen, and Jolie adjusted her stance, ready to take her down if necessary.

She caught sight of their reflection in the mirrors over the vanity and stilled. A part of her shifted away, allowing her to view the scene objectively. The slight short-haired blonde with grim eyes. A bleak expression. The X-ray-thin haggard older woman screaming obscenities, her face and body a silent testament to her lifestyle.

It occurred to Jolie that this was the first time she'd touched her mother since she'd been a child. And the sadness that swept over her nearly made her weep.

"It's my life, ain't it?" Worn out by her struggles, Trixie sagged in Jolie's arms, her breathing heavy and raspy. "Damn cancer's going to kill me anyway. I got a right to choose how I wanna die, don't I?"

Mesmerized by their reflection, Jolie couldn't look away. "I don't think so," she murmured achingly. "I think we get to choose how we're going to live. Dying is out of our hands."

Chapter 8

Special Agent Anthony Dawson took his beeping pager from his pocket and looked at the screen. "Special Agent Truman will be here any minute." Dace glanced up from the surveillance pictures he had spread across the coffee table as the agent rose, stretched and crossed to the kitchen to retrieve his suit jacket from the back of one of the stools.

The man slipped on his suit coat, somehow appearing as fresh as he had that morning. Dace felt a flicker of bemusement. The agent was one of those model-type guys, the kind that could go all day in the same clothes without a crease or a stain. By contrast, Dace would always be a Marine at heart. More at home crawling through the muck on recon than he was in a suit. Once off duty, he changed into jeans and a ratty T-shirt the first chance he got.

But in spite of that flaw, Dawson was all right, as far as feds went. He hadn't balked at sharing some of the background data they were putting together in the investigation. And while Dace didn't kid himself that the agent had been completely forthcoming, it was far more than he would have gotten from Truman.

A light tap sounded on the door. Dawson headed toward it.

"I'd like to keep the file overnight. Discuss it with Jolie."

Dawson paused in his approach to the door. "I suppose that would be all right. If you have Agent Truman bring it in with him in the morning."

"I can do that."

The man nodded and, reaching the door, checked the peephole before unlocking it. "Keep me posted about the convict angle you guys are following. We covered that lead ourselves, of course, but SAC Fenholt will want to be kept apprised of any new developments."

So she could yank the angle from the locals and reassign it to her own unit. Dace kept the cynical words unvoiced. He was well aware of how the feds worked. But if he and Jolie uncovered anything promising, they'd damn well go to Sanders with it first. The chief could flex what muscle he had with the Bureau to make sure they didn't get cut out of the process.

The door opened and Truman entered. He and Dawson engaged in a brief conversation held in undertones before he stepped farther into the room, dropping his garment bag over the back of the couch. "Where's Conrad?"

"She had dinner with her mother." He checked his slim gold wristwatch. "Hawkins called and they're on their way back now. They'll be using the rear entrance."

The other agent frowned. "That was an unnecessary risk, wasn't it?"

Although Dace was inclined to agree with him, Dawson shook his head. "He's decent at evasive driving tactics. Hart joined him at the restaurant. Waller and Reams are on duty outside here this evening. Should be safe enough."

Truman didn't respond as the other agent said his good-byes and left. After locking the door after Dawson, he immediately did a walk-through of the apartment, as if they had unknowingly been harboring the suspect in his absence.

If Dawson was a poster boy for a fed-issued GQ, Truman was his polar opposite. He either wore the same navy suit every time Dace had seen him, or had identical Bureau outfits in his closet. He looked rumpled, tired and ill-tempered. The man might have warranted some sympathy if he weren't such a prick.

As it was, Dace ignored him and scooped up the contents of the file to replace them in the expandable folder. He wouldn't put it past the man to commandeer the information Dawson had left. Although the other agent seemed to be senior, Truman didn't hesitate to voice his disagreements with him over details in the security.

As Dace replaced the last sheet in the folder, Truman re-entered the room and began loosening his tie. "Hope you and Conrad are planning on an early night," he said tersely. "I haven't had more than five hours' sleep at a stretch for over a week. I plan on turning in soon."

Since Dace was sitting on what would be the man's bed, his meaning was clear. He nodded, picked up the file and rose. "I can work upstairs."

But as he ascended the steps, he hesitated. His desk was in the spare room. Jolie's room.

The possessive had him mentally backpedaling. It wasn't *her* room, any more than the couch downstairs was Truman's bed. It was all purely expedient. And temporary. It was his damn house and once this case went down, he'd be alone in it again.

Resolutely, he turned into the second bedroom. His office.

Striding to the desk, he dropped the file on it and pulled out the chair, ignoring the small heap of luggage in the corner.

Other than the bags and some garments in the closet, there was no sign of Jolie's presence. The bed was tucked away back inside the couch. No other personal belongings were in sight. She left, he recalled grimly, a faint wake. When she'd walked out on him before, it was as if she'd never been there at all. Except for the lists he'd run across when he'd moved, there had been no reminders of her left behind.

He immediately tasted the lie. He yanked open the desk drawer with more force than necessary, nearly spilling the contents to the floor. Truth be told, Jolie had carved an indelible mark on him that had taken a long time to erase. Or Sammy had, and she was tied up in his loss. It didn't mean they were destined to repeat their past. He'd never been one to chase the flames after getting burned. Although you couldn't prove it by his behavior a couple nights ago.

His gut clenched at the memory of their kiss. As ideas went, that hadn't ranked up there with his most brilliant. But it was useless to believe that logic had a damn thing to do with it.

He'd spent a lot of months after Jolie left damning her to hell and back. Spent even more months deliberately not thinking of her at all. And, yeah, it rocked him a bit to discover that he could still respond to her on any level.

It was the misery in her eyes that had tugged at him that night. The air of silent tragedy that had always seemed to linger around her. There had been a time when he'd been determined to erase the sadness that could flit so easily across her expression. A short time when he thought he'd succeeded.

He selected a pen and legal pad, shut the drawer. She'd cured him of any underlying protective instincts he'd once had. It would be a cold day in Satan's playground before he'd respond to her again.

With the ease of long habit, he determinedly shoved the woman from his mind. Emptying out the file contents, he started jotting notes that had struck him when he'd first gone over the surveillance photos with Dawson. But there was plenty of other information stuffed in the file that he was eager to delve into, too. He couldn't help but wonder what was included that even Chief Sanders's file lacked.

A good half hour passed before he heard the low murmur of voices downstairs. Jolie had returned. He kept his eyes trained on the updated investigation report. Minutes ticked by. When it finally occurred to him that he'd reread the same page three times without retaining a thing on it, he scowled and summoned his flagging concentration.

But he was hyperaware when her steps sounded on the stairs. Although he didn't look up, he knew precisely when they faltered outside the bedroom door.

"You're working late."

"Convinced Dawson that the file was safe here until Truman delivered it back to him tomorrow." He set his pen down for the moment. "Speaking of Truman…you two getting pretty buddy-buddy? Never heard him speak that long at a stretch before."

Although he hadn't made out their words, hadn't tried to, he was more curious about what the man had to say than he wanted to admit. "Did he open up about the case at all?"

"The case?" Her tone sounded vague as she wandered into the room and perched on the arm of the sofa. "No, not really. Said he was pretty tired. He has an aging father he's been dealing with on his off-nights. Needs to get him placed in an Alzheimer's unit, but that care is pretty pricey. He and his sister are trying to manage on their own for now."

The news startled him on a couple levels. He'd never given Truman's personal life much thought. Or any, to be honest.

He didn't like the guy's attitude, but he was a temporary irritation that would be forgotten as soon as this thing was over.

What was more surprising was that Truman had confided the information to Jolie. Or maybe not so surprising. Her task on an incident response was to draw people out, same as his. She was good at it. It was when it came to reciprocating with bits and pieces about herself that she sucked.

He turned in his chair to look at her and felt a quick punch in his chest. Truman and his problems were forgotten. For someone who had just shared a leisurely meal with her mother, she didn't look particularly relaxed.

She looked brittle. On edge. Like the wrong word could shatter her into a million pieces.

"So. How was dinner?"

"Fine."

Caution reared. She'd been "fine" after Sammy had died, he recalled. "Fine" right up to the point when she'd taken off. Disappeared without another word. *Fine* wasn't necessarily an innocent adjective the way Jolie used it. With her it was a window slammed shut against revealing anything the slightest bit personal about her thoughts or feelings.

And remembering that burned.

"How about your mother?" He wasn't sure why he continued to probe. "Is she fine, too?"

The sudden bleakness that came to her eyes had him instantly regretting his pettiness. "She's dying of cancer. Other than that…she's the same. Exactly the same."

Remorse stabbed him, but before he could fashion an apology—one that was likely to get thrown back in his face—she launched off the sofa and came to his side. "What'd you get from Dawson's file? Anything new?"

Relief coursed through him as she snapped the conversation

back to a purely professional level. Relief, mingled with a tinge
of regret. "Lot more here than what they shared with Sanders."

"Of course." It surprised neither of them. Whatever the
feds shared freely with the locals, they would always hold
plenty back. It was their standard operating procedure.

He picked up the pile of photos gleaned from surveillance
cameras in the last half-dozen bank heists. "Probably two different individuals taking turns being the front man. But
there's a pretty solid link between all the robberies in the MO.
Besides the similarities of the times of day and days of week
that the banks were hit, the suspects took out the surveillance
cameras first, quickly got all the occupants in one place and
filled the bags themselves. If you compare the witness
accounts, the orchestration is the outstanding similarity. Plus,
they used disguises each time and escaped on foot."

The use of disguises was interesting in itself, since better
than sixty percent of bank robbers didn't bother with them.
And these guys weren't the type to simply don ski masks.
Maybe it was the proximity to Hollywood that fired their
imagination. But they were pretty decent makeup artists.
None of the faces in the pictures matched exactly. Foreheads
were raised or lowered, chins rounded or squared, noses
lengthened or shortened, wrinkles added or removed. There
were several slight alterations each time that gave a completely different appearance. It was one more detail that
pointed at the pair as professionals.

And successful. They'd gotten away with better than thirty
million so far.

The lights snapped off downstairs. Dace nudged the door
shut with his foot.

Each photo was stamped with the date. Jolie studied the
most recent one the longest. "John," the HT, could pass for
a slightly older-than-average college student.

She echoed his thoughts. "Based on this and other photos, he could be anywhere between twenty-five and thirty-five."

"And the other subject could be a decade or more older. But that's not what I found most interesting in the file. It was this." Dace picked up a stapled report and handed it to her. She began skimming.

Without waiting for her to finish, Dace continued with what had been bothering him all night. "That report summarizes what Dawson told me they'd concluded from the examination of the devices. Because they're improvised explosive devices, they're going on the assumption that they're dealing with an amateur with some expertise. But one of the wit statements from the incident last week, from Tyler's mother, claims she heard the HT talking to someone early in the incident while they were in the vault. Thought he called the person Loomer. Goomer. Boomer. She wasn't sure. But she thought she heard him say, '…up to you, Loomer.'"

Jolie looked up, her interest arrested. "He could have gotten out on a cell phone before the grid was shut down. Maybe more than once. It would explain the well-orchestrated rescue attempt."

Impatience filled him. "Yeah, and we can be sure the feds are running the name and all its variations through every database they can access. But what if she didn't hear a *name*, exactly? What if it was a call sign?"

"Boomer?"

He nodded, satisfied that she'd followed the same mental path he'd taken.

"That would put us back to our original impression when we were talking to the HT." Jolie slowly sank to the floor to sit cross-legged, in a boneless movement he couldn't have imitated if he tried.

"That he had military or law enforcement training or knowledge. Yeah."

She tapped the edge of the report against her open palm. "Given our near-death experience in my parking lot, the accomplice must be the one with the explosive expertise. Great."

"Maybe not. If it's just a nickname, sure. But if we're correct, and it's a call sign, or given by someone familiar with call signs, the subject got hung with it for making a less than intelligent move. *Blondie 2-0.*"

Her murderous glare did nothing to erase the smirk from his lips. The story of how she'd earned her call sign stemmed from her actions on a response five years earlier that had been roundly summarized as a "blond moment."

"You really want to reminisce about how we earned our call signs, *Hootch?*"

He winced. Since he wasn't anxious to recall his unfortunate run-in with a K-9 bomb-sniffing dog his first month on the unit, he said, "No use being mean. I might not even have considered the name being a call sign if something didn't bother me about those explosives."

She cocked her head, her searing blue gaze fixed on him, and for a moment his mind went blank. Those damn eyes of hers should be declared illegal. He pushed the chair back from the desk to give himself some room to stretch out his legs. And to collect his thoughts, which had scattered like confetti in a windstorm.

"I've told you that I'm veteran Marine Recon."

She nodded. They'd talked about it before. Swift. Silent. Deadly. The words and the 3rd Reconnaissance Battalion skull logo were tattooed on his left bicep. His military background had led him to volunteer for the first SWAT unit formed by Metro City PD, six years ago. "There's nothing in the files about the link to the terrorist cell, so we can't judge the validity of the lead ourselves. But you and I both know that with the Bureau the past few years, it's all terrorism, all the time. And given the Homeland Security involvement… they're going to chase that angle down to the last man."

"You think they're blinded to other possibilities?"

"Not following them as vigorously, maybe. Take these IEDs. They look at them and see similarities to those used by terrorists in the Middle East. I'm saying there are other explanations."

"Could be self-taught. I could name half a dozen sites on the Internet where they sell books on that very subject," Jolie offered.

He shook his head. "Nine out of ten amateurs making explosives at their kitchen table end up nursing bloody stumps. The surveillance photos show both subjects with hands and fingers intact. Believe me, I went over the report on the explosive devices with a fine-tooth comb. Special Ops soldiers get intensive instruction in makeshift weaponry, and how to combat it. Al Qaeda operatives aren't the only ones who would know how to use that weaponry. When I was on active duty, part of our training would be to go up against an OPFOR troop. Their job was to lie in ambush, or launch an attack using the same weapons and tactics used by the terrorists."

He appreciated the quick flicker of comprehension on her face. Jolie was never one he had to spend time explaining things to. "And OPFOR troops are still used?"

Inclining his head, he said, "They play a vital role in in-struction."

She leaned forward slightly. "During negotiations we thought law enforcement or military background was a possibility. Someone with fairly recent military service could have been OPFOR in Iraq. Afghanistan."

"And these surveillance photos, as worthless as they are for ID purposes, do show that one of the subjects is older than the other."

"If we're still thinking that one of them did time, he'd likely be the older one," Jolie mused, unfolding her legs. "Which would mean the HT is ex-military."

"Possibly even ex-Special Forces," he corrected, his tone grim. The thought of a soldier trained to defend his country going rogue and using those skills against it was as sour as suspecting a cop had gone bad.

"Well, I can see why the feds aren't pursuing this connection," she said, her tone wry.

"If they've thought of it," he interjected.

"It's shaky."

"Yep."

His cheerful agreement didn't ease her thoughtful expression. "We've got that list of paroled ex-cons with bank robbery records. But without a way to cross-reference that with a list of military personnel who went inactive around the same time…"

He was way ahead of her. "But what if we could access those names?"

She narrowed her gaze at him. He had a distant thought that the case had distracted her enough to wipe away some of the earlier bleakness from her expression. "And just how would we do that? The government databases aren't going to highlight which former military had that kind of training."

"No. But I've got a Marine buddy who ended up at OMPF/PERMS. The electronic records management system for the military personnel files," he explained, seeing her blank expression. "Every individual in the military has a file and all duties except for the most classified would be in-cluded. It wouldn't take him any time at all. But it'll end up costing me, one way or another." The last time his buddy Ben Stratton had accessed some information for him, it had cost Dace a couple of Cardinals tickets. It had been a small price to pay to close the homicide investigation he'd been working.

When he glanced at Jolie again, there was a small satis-fied smile curling her lips. The sight hit him like a fast left jab to the solar plexus. He remembered that smile. Remem-bered her wearing it and nothing else as she sat astride him, controlling their movements until he'd been sweating and shaking, his control frayed. The memory torched something inside him, an inner heat that made his forehead dampen.

"Are you thinking what I'm thinking?"

He seriously doubted it. Shifting to a more comfortable position, he ordered his flagging concentration back to the case. "What?"

"We know the feds would have looked at recent parolees with bank robbery sheets first. No doubt they've run them upside down and sideways. But now they're focusing on the terrorism angle. By following this lead, we may be able to uncover something before they even get around to kicking over the same rocks."

"If we get lucky." Her enthusiasm was contagious. They'd never worked a case together before. Had never been assigned to the same precinct. But they seemed to share a wavelength. He felt as comfortable bouncing ideas off her as he did with Jack, whom he'd known since they'd both been rookies. "We make a good team."

Her expression shuttered. She handed him the wit report to place back in the file and rose. "Better team on the job than off it, I'd say."

The reference to their past had his temper flaring, quick

and hot. In a dim corner of his mind he recognized that the anger was too close to the surface after all this time. Too easily summoned. "Is it really that easy for you, Jolie? Push it aside, don't think about it. Encounter a problem and, hey, just walk away and forget about it, right?"

"Easy?" Like him, she kept her voice low, but her laugh was bitter, her eyes hot. "When was anything ever *easy* between us? Our biggest mistake was in thinking we could turn what we had into something more. Before you came along, I knew what my boundaries were." She thumped her fist against her chest for emphasis. "I accepted them. You think it was easy to ignore a lifetime of caution and reach for something that was never meant to be? It wasn't smart. And it sure as hell wasn't *easy*. Neither was living with what happened because I forgot the danger of wanting *more*."

Her sudden fury blindsided him. She was a master at keeping her feelings locked behind a veneer of control. Her outburst offered a rare glimpse into the thoughts she kept so tightly guarded. His temper faded as he focused on what she'd just revealed. "Why's it a danger, Jolie?" His voice was as nonthreatening as he used with HTs. "What's so bad about wanting the kind of life other people have?"

With eyes flat and hard, she retorted, "Because I'm not like other people. You know what happened at my fourth foster home if we reached for more at the dinner table? We got a leather strap across the back of our hands. It didn't take long to get the message. Accept what you've got and be happy with it."

...*my fourth foster home*... He filed the words away to be examined later. She was still talking. Pacing the small confines of the room.

"I'm a good cop. Good on HNT." She shot him a humorless smile. "Believe me, I know what my limitations are.

My biggest mistake was allowing you to convince me to set them aside."

That was a sharp, jagged pain in his heart. "What are you saying? That Sammy was a mistake? That you wished you'd never gone through with the pregnancy?"

The anguish on her face made her earlier misery pale in comparison. "You don't get it, do you? I don't regret Sammy. How could I? But you screwed up bigger than I did. Your mistake wasn't in wanting a child.

"It was wanting me to be its mother."

Chapter 9

Jolie couldn't breathe. Not with Dace watching her with that arrested expression, as if she'd just verbalized something he'd been thinking. Knowing the truth didn't mean she was ready to hear him agree with it.

"You don't think you were meant to be a mother." His careful rephrasing of her words had her raising a hand.

"Don't try HNT active listening now, Dace. Not on me." Because looking at him made it difficult to think, she half turned away, focused on the heap of luggage on the floor. She needed to get some sleep. Summon unconsciousness that would let her forget at least for a while. And if she had to rely on one of those pills the doctor had pressed on her at the hospital to beckon slumber, well, there were worse crutches.

"Maybe you think I wasn't meant to be a father either."

"I never thought that." Seeing him with his family, his mother and sisters, nieces and nephews, had always made her feel like a child with her nose pressed against the window of a candy store. His relationship with his family was easy, natural, born of long familiarity and a deep-seated love. And although they'd all been kind to her, she'd always felt out of place around them. The boisterous teasing, the commotion of family get-togethers, the openly curious remarks had all felt slightly suffocating. She'd faced down armed gunmen with barely a flicker of emotion, but one of Dace's upcoming family events would tie her stomach in knots for days beforehand.

"So this is all about you. Things would have been different if it had been Sheila who had gotten pregnant. Or Lindsey. Or Meredith."

The names of his former girlfriends had her flinching, a buried reaction from the time when she'd had a right to feel jealousy. But she couldn't dodge the truth in his words. "Yes."

"That is such crap, Jolie."

The change in his tone had her head whipping around to face him. There was incredulity in his expression, heat in his eyes. "We both read the research. We hadn't done anything to increase Sammy's risk of SIDS. His death was tragic. But it wasn't our fault. It wasn't yours, just because you happened to be the one to find him."

A sliver of pain lodged deep at the reminder. They'd alternated shifts so one of them could be home with Sammy as much as possible. Dace had left the house forty minutes earlier on the day she'd awakened and checked on their son. On the day she found him not breathing in the crib they'd selected with such care. The memory of that morning still throbbed like a wound.

"He wouldn't have been any less dead if you'd had first shift that day instead of me. Or would you have blamed me, if the situation was reversed?"

"Of course not!" The denial was out of her mouth before she could consider the words.

He gave a nod. "Of course not. But it's okay to blame yourself. That makes no sense at all."

She struggled to keep her voice pitched low. How incongruous that the first real discussion they'd had about their son's death was held in near-whispers with a sleeping federal agent downstairs. "I don't blame myself for Sammy's death." She didn't, exactly. What she deserved blame for was tempting fate. For reaching for something she'd known better than to hope for. "You don't get it. I did everything right." There was a catch in that last word and she stopped, waited for her voice to steady before continuing. "I stopped smoking as soon as soon as I knew I was pregnant." Even before she'd decided to go through with the pregnancy. And that implication was particularly elusive.

"I followed all the rules." She heard the plaintive note in her voice, was helpless to temper it. She'd thought she could shore up her complete ignorance about babies by reading everything she could lay her hands on. Making lists of things to remember. Careful notes on what to avoid. But education was no match for lack of instinct. And there she'd failed miserably. "You had to show me everything."

She didn't hear him move. But suddenly he was behind her, his hands on her shoulders. Slowly, inexorably, he overcame the resistance in her body to draw her back against his chest. "My experience with diaper changing wasn't exactly something I came by willingly." His voice was in her ear, tinged with humor. "My sisters' offspring have all perfected the art of instant elimination the moment their parents walk out the door."

That surprised a laugh from her, and a bit of tension eased from her body. He rested his chin lightly on the top of her head. His arms slid down her arms to link around her waist. "Inexperience didn't make you a bad mother. It wasn't some kind of sign from the fates when your milk didn't come in, and we used bottles instead of breast-feeding. It just *was*. You can't read hidden meanings into things neither of us could control. We stumbled through the first few weeks after Sammy was born the same way most new parents do. Scared to death and in a sleep-deprived fog."

She gave a short laugh again, a part of her amazed that the memories could bring as much comfort as pain. She let her head rest against his chest. Heard the reassuring steady thud of his heartbeat. "I don't think you slept for the first three days after his birth." Exhaustion had worked on her, but Dace had been alert to every hitch in Sammy's breathing. Every squeak heard over the baby monitor.

"Well, I eventually perfected the art of pretending not to hear him wake up, didn't I?"

She pinched one of his arms, satisfied when she felt him flinch. "You did become quite masterful at that, yes." She hadn't ever really minded. There had been a rare peace in the times she'd spent rocking her son as she fed him. And if it had never stopped feeling a bit foreign, there had also been joy in those quiet times she'd never regret.

Dace still didn't understand. The certainty pierced her heart. He could probably only fully comprehend once he'd met Trixie. But even knowing that didn't stem the surge of desire. He was a protector to the core, a cop, with that Marine toughness as much a part of him as his eye color. Maybe that was why his unexpected tenderness could so easily undo her.

She turned in his arms, tipped her chin up to look at him. The strong stubborn jaw was stubbled, the scrape already healing. His chestnut hair was ruffled, probably from his habit of jamming his fingers through it when he was poring over case notes. But it was what she saw in his shockingly green eyes that had her pulse stuttering.

Desire.

A smoky tendril of heat suffused her. She spent her life exerting control. Over her emotions. Her environment. Her relationships. But her body made a mockery of that restraint as it softened against his. A shrill of alarm sounded in the recesses of her mind. It would be a mistake to forget all the pain in their relationship and focus on the purely carnal satisfaction she could find with him.

Their gazes tangled. Her throat abruptly dried. If memory served, when it came to carnal satisfaction, they'd been pretty damn combustible. He stroked a lazy path up her spine, and she shuddered in response. Now was the time to heed caution and step away, before there were any more regrets between them.

His head dipped, and his teeth closed over the cord of her neck, testing not quite painfully. Reason clouded. They knew where all the mines were buried in their relationship, didn't they? Surely they could sidestep them to focus on the parts that were separate from the regret. Dace was no more anxious than she to relive the pain of their past.

But this aspect of it… She dragged her lips along his jaw, felt the scrape of whiskers against her mouth and the sensation cemented her decision. He was the only man who'd ever made her feel like this. Want like this. It wasn't the frankly sexual passion between them that was to be feared. It was fooling themselves that it could be more.

His lips moved over hers then and there was a flare in the pit of her belly, hot and immediate. He knew how to kiss a woman, deep and devastating. With a single-minded intensity that had the rest of the world dimming. Inner fires flaring. She opened her mouth beneath his and dove into the flames.

His flavor was dark temptation, lethal to her senses. She

slid her hands inside his T-shirt to skate up hard-muscled sides, her fingers flexing in remembered pleasure. She'd always enjoyed the contrasts of them, his sinewy strength against her softness. And she'd enjoyed stripping him of that strength, torching his control until desperation turned his breathing ragged, his hands hard and frantic.

He cupped her face in his palms, but there was nothing gentle in the gesture. His mouth devoured hers, their tongues tangling, breath mingling, teeth clashing. Swinging her around, he walked her backward until she felt the wall at her shoulders, and still he didn't lift his mouth from hers. Her muscles melted, hot wax under a molten flame. Here was the hunger she remembered. The hint of savagery that called forth an answering wildness.

He urged her legs apart with his knee, then stepped between them. His erection pressed against her belly and she squirmed against him, wanting to feel him where she was empty and aching. As if aware of her frustration, his hands went to her butt and he lifted her. With her legs locked around his hips, she rocked against his hardness, feeling his reaction even if she couldn't manage to drag her eyes open to watch it.

With sudden urgency, Jolie bunched his shirt in her fists, dragged it up his torso. Dace finally moved his mouth from hers long enough to rid himself of the garment. Her head lolled against the wall, her fingers dancing over the remembered planes of his chest, the hollows beneath his ribs. The ridges of bone and sinew.

She felt his fingers on the fastenings of her shirt and her breath caught. Held. There was something exquisitely sensuous about focusing on touch alone. The languid slipping of one button from its hole. The inch of exposed flesh bathed by Dace's clever wicked tongue. Another button. Skin prickling in anticipation of his lips long seconds before it, too, was tasted.

He took his time. Each button was released with exquisite care. Each bared expanse of flesh meticulously explored. Jolie forgot about her own exploration, the teasing journey she'd been mapping along his biceps, across his chest. She clutched at his shoulders, fingers digging into his flesh, and shivered each time his mouth found a new square of flesh to map through taste alone.

This rollicking in her pulse was familiar, but no less heady for it. Every brush of his lips, every teasing slide of his tongue was a dark promise of pleasures to come. But it also fueled a quiet desperation in her system. She wanted to feel him, all of him. Flesh against flesh. Their bodies sealed so closely that not even a breath of air could fit between them. And she wanted him quaking, too. Wanted to unleash the primitive nature he battled to keep leashed. She wanted, quite frankly, to strip him of every defense, even as he stripped her of clothes.

To that end, she relaxed her fingers, went on a quest designed to unharness his control. He released her fourth button and her senses scattered when his tongue delved into her cleavage, danced along the top of her bra where flesh met lace. It took all the strength she could muster to concentrate on finding the places that made him shudder. The soft velvety skin beneath his arms. A fingernail scraping over one male nipple.

And the feel of his touch faltering, the hiss of his breath sucked in was its own reward.

Her reach was constrained by their position but she was thorough in her investigation. She brushed her fingers over his back, feeling the flesh punctuated by vertebrae. The muscles beneath her fingers quivered under her touch like an impatient stallion's.

His hands began to hurry a bit as he pulled her shirt up to undo the bottom buttons. With one practiced movement he released the front clasp of her bra and spread the fabric aside.

Her nipples were knotted, awaiting his touch. And when it didn't immediately come, Jolie managed to drag her eyes open, a demand on her lips.

It went unuttered. Dace was staring at her, and she felt seared by his gaze. It painted her face, her breasts, causing her nipples to tighten even more. The look was a little possessive, slightly cruel, a man surveying a woman he meant to take at his leisure. She knew from experience he'd pleasure and take pleasure in return, and that knowledge sparked comets of heat through her veins.

Eyes locked on him, she arched her back, a carnal invitation, and watched the color slash across his cheekbones. His jaw tightened. Intuitively she knew he was battling against the urge to rush the ending, an urge she wouldn't protest. But she saw the moment he won the battle, saw the slight curve to his lips as he reached out a finger to brush it lightly over her nipples.

She jerked against him in involuntary response, and her reaction seemed to ignite something inside him. He slid a hand up to cup one of her breasts, capturing the taut bud between thumb and forefinger, before lowering his mouth to take the other nipple between his lips.

Kaleidoscopic colors wheeled behind her eyelids. Jolie leaned back while pressing closer against him, and he responded to her unspoken demand by suckling strongly from her. The slight scrape of teeth against her flesh had hunger leaping forth like an uncaged tiger. Her earlier plan to make him ache, make him *need* was forgotten. Her fingers twisted in his hair, urging him to take more.

She was a master at maintaining her guard, lest she reveal vulnerabilities it had taken her a lifetime to hide. But unlike any other man she'd ever met, Dace could dismantle that guard with mind-numbing ease. That fact had always dismayed and alarmed her by turn. But the flip side was that he could get closer, could make her *feel* things no one else ever had. Still frightening. Terrifying, even. But also rewarding because her physical response to him was just as keen.

He lifted his mouth, and the cooler air tightened her nipple almost painfully. She met his lips with her own, all pretense stripped away. She felt alive again in his arms. Desperately, achingly alive. And the heat careening through her veins warmed where she'd been cold and empty for too long. There was a claim sometimes leveled at SWAT units that they were adrenaline junkies. Maybe that explained her reaction to Dace. There was danger here—a history fraught with complications and heartbreak. But sensation heightened unbearably everywhere they touched. Pulse points were sharpened to razor-edged keenness.

When he swung her into his arms, she opened her eyes dazedly, her wits completely dulled by the passion-induced fog. Dace moved toward the door, flicked off the light and was striding down the hall before she quite knew what was happening.

He glanced down at her as he carried her through the doorway to his room, pushing the door closed behind him with his foot. But if he was waiting for an objection, he wasn't going to get one from her.

Jolie trailed the nail of her index finger over his shoulder, down his defined bicep, over to his chest to trace a teasing circle around one flat nipple. His eyes slitted in response, and a small smile curled her lips. She leaned upward to nip at his collarbone before he opened his arms and she found herself falling.

Dace had her stripped almost by the time she hit the mattress. Following her down on the bed, his arms framed her body, his mouth demanding on hers. The room was shrouded in darkness. But there was a slash of moonlight slanting through the blinds, painting the bed with a wide pearly glimmer. It sheened his body with an otherworldly glow that furthered the sense of intimacy. The black velvet shadows wrapped them in a sensual cocoon that kept the rest of the world at bay, swept aside the past.

There was just sensation. The stroking of his healing palms over her skin, hot and demanding on her curves, gentle on her wounded leg. The contrast kept her off-kilter, her emotions swinging between lust and tenderness.

An alarm shrilled in the recesses of her mind. *Danger.* There was a risk in feeling anything deeper than the need to assuage the savage hunger clawing through her system. Dace trailed a finger up her leg, circled teasingly around the heat centered between her thighs, and the inner warning bells were silenced. Her life had been full of denying herself any indulgence. She wasn't going to deny herself this.

Dace leaned in for a kiss. Deep. Wet. Rawly carnal. His palm covered her mound, which was damp and aching. He sent his tongue in search of hers at the same time he parted her slick folds and entered her with one exploring finger.

Her hips arched, twisting beneath him at the dual assault. Her blood was churning in her veins, frothing and crashing like white water. There was primitive demand in his kiss. In his touch. It was a demand she reciprocated.

Jolie's hands streaked over his body, tempting, teasing, reveling in the sensual warmth of sleek skin covering sinew and muscle. He moved his leg over one of hers, as if to hold her in place, and she was reminded that he was still half dressed.

There was something intensely vulnerable about lying naked beneath a man who was still clothed. She'd never allowed herself to feel vulnerable with any other man. Not even this much. Her fingers trailed along the flesh above his waistband, felt his stomach muscles quiver beneath her touch and knew she wasn't the only one susceptible to these sensations.

He parted her legs and eased another finger inside her, catching her bottom lip with his teeth as he intensified the sensual assault. She dragged her eyelids open, caught his eyes on hers. Knowing. Slightly predatory. It was a game they'd played before, each intent on being the first to drive the other just a little crazy.

She unfastened his jeans, scraping her thumbnail down his zipper, pressing lightly against the hard length of him straining beneath the fabric. She saw him swallow a groan. Then he found the taut cluster of nerves between her legs and began a slow rhythmic circling.

Her vision grayed, sensation arrowing straight to her womb. It took a great deal of effort to continue the game, to gather her scattered senses and work the zipper of his jeans down. Slow. Excruciatingly slow. One tooth at a time.

His touch became more urgent. He lowered his head, took a beaded nipple between his teeth and worried it gently. But there was nothing gentle about her response. Her back arched off the mattress. She had always been far more impatient than he. Anticipation, she thought, was vastly overrated.

She felt him smile against her breast, and the gesture of male satisfaction acted to steel her resolve. Pushing his jeans open, she reached inside them to squeeze his hardness and felt his body jerk involuntarily against hers.

It was her turn to smile. But a moment later a moan escaped her lips as he began to stroke his fingers inside her more insistently, his thumb pressing more firmly. Her body was betraying her.

With a shaking hand, she pushed aside his formfitting briefs to take his warm, pulsing erection in her fingers. She had time for one lingering stroke before he lifted his head from her breast, caught her hand in one of his. He pinned it on the pillow beside her head, his other hand never pausing in its sensual ministrations.

"Not…fair," she gasped. Her muscles tightened as she struggled against giving in to the vortex of desire, sucking her in to the inevitable conclusion.

Placing a stinging kiss below her ear, he murmured, "When have you ever known me to play fair?"

She couldn't summon an answer. Sensation slammed against sensation. There was an urgency in his touch, a demand. And while she could fight the sensual assault, the conclusion couldn't be denied.

He was saying something else, his voice a ragged whisper. But the sound slipped away, as evasive as wisps of fog. Nerve endings spiraled to concentrate where he was touching her so intimately. Her control tenuous. Teetering.

And then it snapped and she shattered, falling headlong into a pleasure too long denied.

Breath panting and uneven, she was aware of his movements beside her, swift and jerky. She heard a slight sound, realized he was donning protection and the realization had reason returning.

But then he was beside her again, sleek, lean naked flesh a temptation she couldn't resist. And the longing, just satiated, began to climb again.

She leaned over him, intent on mapping his body with her lips, one inch at a time. But now he was the eager one. His muscles quivering with tension, he urged her astride him, his eyes dark with passion. The skin over his cheekbones was drawn tight.

She rose above him, guiding his entry, and then he hesitated. His face lay half in moonlight, half in shadow. But she saw the sheen of perspiration on his forehead. Felt his muscles bunched beneath her. Then she moved, taking him inside in one long stroke, and the tether on his restraint snapped.

Her hips were clutched in hard desperate fingers as he urged her to a faster pace. And while minutes earlier she'd been intent on teasing, torturing, now she found herself as hungry as he. She braced her hands on his shoulders and met every lunge of his hips, each a little more desperate than the last.

The position felt familiar. So was the hot avid gaze he pinned her with as they strained together. Her blood began to pulse again, scorching rivers under her skin. Need coiled in her belly. And the urgent pace he set was familiar, too. Familiar and welcome.

As she saw his face pass into the light, then back into shadow, there was a moment when the past and present melded so completely she couldn't separate the two. It caused an instant of panic, nebulous, but just as quickly dissipated by the urgency of their movements.

The rhythm quickened. Breath shortened. The climax shook her first, startling in its intensity. In the throes of her own pleasure she felt Dace finish and melted, bonelessly, when she heard him groan a word that almost sounded like her name.

That sliver of moonlight was keeping Dace awake. He should get up, adjust the blinds, but he couldn't summon the energy.

He stroked Jolie's hip, one arm curved around her to keep her close. She'd always slept deeply after great sex. And the sex, he recalled, had always been mind-blowingly great.

It was when they were out of bed that problems evolved.

Because he didn't want to examine the sneaky little doubts that were circling in his mind, he pushed them aside. There were other, more pressing things to concentrate on. Like what Jolie had revealed earlier.

Four foster homes. Probably more, the way she'd phrased it. He kept his touch light as he traced patterns on her skin, staring sightlessly at the ceiling. She hadn't ever told him much about her past prior to joining the force, but apparently most of what she had told him had been a lie.

That should piss him off. It *did* piss him off. But it also explained a hell of a lot, and he'd waited a long time for an explanation. Now he had at least part of one, and he could guess at the rest. It didn't change anything but at least he could start to understand. Would understand better when he could pry more out of her.

But it didn't matter. He told himself that and tried to believe it. The past was past. Over. Just like they were over, in any way other than the physical.

But if it didn't matter, he'd release her. Let her roll away and curl up into a ball, the way she always slept if allowed to. Alone, even when someone else was lying beside her.

And he *would* release her. In a minute. Maybe two.

It was the cop in him, he reasoned, his eyes on that slice of light dividing the shadows of the room. He was used to piecing together puzzles to see the whole. Trained to look for answers. But he hadn't looked very damn hard when they'd been together, or he'd have known all about Jolie's mother. All about her childhood. All about the demons that had shaped her fears, fueled her doubts. That was what had him lying here awake.

She stirred against him and his hand stilled, waiting until she gave a little sigh before she went motionless again. The warning signs had been there three years ago. It wasn't that he hadn't seen them. He hadn't pried with Jolie because he hadn't wanted to face whatever it was that had made those defenses so much a part of her. It had been so much easier to tear them down, smash through them.

His hand went to her spine, tracing the vertebrae there, so delicate to hide a will so strong. He'd spent a year and a half blaming her for walking away. Sixteen months trying to forget her altogether. It was pretty damn bitter to lie here realizing just how big a hand he'd played in their misery.

Adam Marker pulled the door open, cocked a brow when he saw the newcomer. "Don't you sleep?"

"Not much, thanks to you." Gee walked in, glancing at Mose sitting at the table, drinking his way through a twelve-pack. "The news is all over the media." Tightly controlled fury was in every word. "What the hell did you do?"

"Me and Mose went hunting, is all." Adam watched Gee look over at the high-powered rifle lying on the table in front of Mose. "Open season. Bagged us a couple more SWATs. Those cowboys will all be pissing their pants when word gets out."

And there was a vicious stab of satisfaction at the thought. Freaking cops would all be dead before he was through. Every one of them that had David's blood on their hands. He wouldn't stop until they were all as cold and lifeless as his brother.

"You're out of control. Killing two more of the SWAT unit is going to make this more difficult, don't you get that? You need to get your head out of your ass. Nothing you do is going to bring David back. You're just digging a hole for us we can't hope to get out of. Call it even, pull up stakes and head to another state before you bring this whole thing down on us."

"What have you been smoking?" Mose tittered at Adam's retort, the sound abruptly trailing off when Gee threw him a glare. "The memorial service is the day after tomorrow. We're prepared. You just need to do your part to ensure that nothing goes wrong." Gee's constant second-guessing was wearing on his nerves. But then, everything got on his nerves these days. The waiting, especially. The constant news stories about the freaking cops who had died at the bank.

There'd be new stories for the media to feed on after the night he and Mose had spent. He hadn't missed this time. He'd remembered everything David had told him. Hadn't rushed the shots. Kept his breathing nice and slow. A slow easy squeeze on the trigger.

But already the pleasure from the kills was fading. For every one he'd managed to kill, there were more out there deserving death. He wanted them all. Only then would David be avenged.

"You think you're running this operation?" Gee took three quick strides and had Adam around the neck before he thought to react. "Think I can't bury your ass before you even have a chance to wonder what hit you? One phone call from me and you'll have a pass right back to prison. But it would be death row this time. You really that anxious to join your brother in hell?"

Adam let the fingers close around his windpipe. He waited. Calm. Deadly calm. Felt his breathing catch and labor as those fingers started to squeeze. Then watched Gee still when Mose stuck the tip of the M40's muzzle beneath one ear.

He reached up, pried Gee's fingers off him and shoved away. "I think you could say there's been a shift in the balance of leadership. You try to double-cross me and you'll never see us coming for you. Might be a bullet." Mose punctuated his words with a little jab of the barrel. "Might be a big bang and then nothing left of you but pieces."

He turned away, went to the window. Dawn was spreading sticky pink smudges across the horizon. Metro City was slowly awakening. "You do your part. Follow the plan. We'll take out as many as we can."

"And then we get back to business?"

Still too much demand in Gee's voice for Adam's liking, but he lifted a shoulder. "Let's wait until after the memorial. Then we can talk about business."

Chapter 10

"Detective Riley was shot as he was grilling in his backyard."

Chief Sanders looked like he'd aged ten years in the past few days. Jolie watched him at the podium of the conference room, feeling as shell-shocked as the rest of the occupants of the room looked. "Officer Fitzpatrick was killed getting out of his car in his driveway after work. Two hours between attacks, but with only about ten miles between the two locations, the same subject could easily have made both shots. No spent cartridges were left behind. But I'm guessing the slugs retrieved in the autopsies will match. Just like they'll match the ones they took out of Carter, Laeten and Thompson."

He looked out at the remaining members of the unit assembled before him. The silence in the space was deafening. "I don't think I have to tell you, this is unprecedented in the MCPD. You've all been on your guard." His slitted gaze traveled around the room, touching on each individual. "All

been extra careful, and still we're losing officers. Good people,
with families. I'm not willing to lose any more."

"I say you turn us loose to do some hunting of our own,"
someone called out. There was a murmur of agreement
among the officers, one that the chief silenced with an
upraised palm.

"Believe me, I understand the sentiment. But I'm not
allowing this dirtbag to use the rest of this unit for target
practice. As of this moment, you are all on paid leave."

Jolie heard Dace utter a low oath. His was seemingly the
mildest response in the room. The officers were all voicing
protests, loudly. Even Lewis and Mendel were joining in.

"With all due respect, Chief…" Lewis stood, pitching his
voice above the din. "The cost to the city will be astronomi-
cal. Don't you think we could be put to better use joining in
the search for these guys?"

"Let me worry about the cost to the city, Captain." But
Jolie could tell from the chief's expression that the words had
scored. Counting her and Dace, nearly thirty people were
affected. The city council didn't even like paying officers over-
time. They sure weren't going to be happy about approving
extra leave.

The verbal dissent in the room intensified. "This is not up
for debate!" he roared into the microphone. Slowly, sullenly,
the officers quieted. "I want each and every one of you to
leave town, and that is an order. If you haven't already moved
your families, take them with you. You'll be relieved of duty
for the next forty-eight hours, at which time you will call your
precinct lieutenant and ask for further instructions. Captains
Lewis and Mendel, you will see that every person on your
squads follows those orders before you vacate the city your-
selves. Lewis, you'll see that Carter is apprised of her new
orders. You're all excused."

Judging from the mutinous expressions on the unit members' faces, there wasn't an agreeable person in the room. Jolie wondered how many of them would directly defy the chief's order. It went against any cop's nature to tuck tail and run in the face of a threat. She'd much prefer the task she and Dace had undertaken. But was Sanders backing off their involvement, too?

As if in answer to her silent question, Sanders turned at the door, scanned the room. "Recker. Conrad. Come with me." With a slanted look in Dace's direction, Jolie rose as he did and complied.

They trailed him down the hall in the direction of his offices. "He's going to shut down our part in the operation," Dace muttered. "Have your arguments lined up and ready. I'm not pulling out of this now. Not with the memorial scheduled for tomorrow."

Jolie nodded. The media had been broadcasting updates about the memorial for days. And there had been strategic mention of the fact that two of the fallen policemen's fellow officers would be on the dais representing the entire unit.

She was going to be on that dais. *Needed* to be there, now more than ever.

Sanders was behind his desk when they arrived. He didn't invite them to sit down. "Close the door." He waited for Dace to comply before leveling them with a shrewd gaze. "My gut is telling me to send you two packing along with the others. Despite the best efforts of the Bureau and the department, there's no way your safety can be guaranteed. Given the events in the past twenty-four hours, I'm thinking the risk may be too great."

"I think that would be a mistake, sir."

His tone sharpening, he glared at Jolie. "Really?"

Thinking fast, she injected a reasonable tone to her voice. "With the rest of the unit gone, it's more imperative than ever that we go through with the original plan for tomorrow.

This guy isn't going to be able to resist the temptation the memorial presents. He's going to have to leave the area soon. The investigation has got to be pressuring him. He'll show up tomorrow. He won't be able to help himself."

He surveyed her from beneath beetled brows. "That's your professional opinion?"

"Yes, sir. Whoever the HT was, there was a close relationship with the accomplice. This guy is a brother, father… someone who feels guilt at the HT's death. Someone compelled to avenge it."

He shifted his attention to Dace. "What do you think, Recker?"

"This may be our only shot to catch this guy," Dace said bluntly. "He's planning something for tomorrow. We can use bomb-sniffing dogs. Set up double perimeters. Entrench our own snipers. The feds will have a stable of agents there."

"As we will."

Dace inclined his head. "It's as safe as it can be. Safer than Riley and Fitzpatrick were. You can't keep the squad on leave indefinitely. This is really the only good option we have."

He took a step forward, lowered his voice. "However, I think we can minimize our risk, sir, if just one of us appears tomorrow at the memorial."

It took a moment for the import of his words to sink in. When they did, Jolie's temper instantly spiked. She lodged a discreet elbow in his ribs, to no noticeable affect. He continued. "Detective Conrad can stay behind with the protection offered by the Bureau, and I can appear onstage alone."

"I think second-guessing our strategy is wasted effort at this point," she quickly said from between gritted teeth. "I volunteered for this duty and I haven't changed my mind in the time since."

"Well, I haven't decided whether to change *my* mind,"

Sanders snapped. "No chief likes to bury his officers. I'm not willing to take the chance on two more funerals."

"This is the best opportunity we're going to get to draw him out," Jolie said quietly. "If we succeed, this thing is over. The rest of the unit is safe. It's a risk worth taking, sir. I'm willing to take it."

Sanders's mouth was a hard, flat line. He took his time answering and every second of silence that ticked by was an eternity. Finally he said, "I have a meeting with Fenholt in an hour. I'll let you know my decision by the end of the day. In the meantime, you can get back to the investigation." His attention drifted to a pile of paperwork before him on the desktop.

Releasing a breath she hadn't realized she'd been holding, Jolie nodded. "Thank you, sir."

"Don't thank me yet, Conrad," he said tersely. "Either you're getting pulled off this detail or I'm going to allow them to dangle you out there on that stage like a sitting duck. Either way, gratitude is the last damn thing you should be feeling right now."

"You jerk." Suppressed anger lengthened her strides, allowing her to easily keep up with Dace. "You cheating low-life sneak. Where the hell do you get off trying to bump me from this detail? I was the one who volunteered in the first place. You're the tagalong."

Dace's lack of response was even more maddening. She reached out and grabbed his arm, pulling him to a stop. "I'm a cop, just like you. I do the same job, take the same risks. You undermined me in there. Don't *ever* do that again."

He just looked at her, his expression impassive. "You done?"

Incensed, she clenched her fist, fought the urge to take a swing at him. "I'm just getting started, ace. If there will be only one of us up there tomorrow, it's going to be me. I want your promise that you'll drop this end run you're trying to do around me."

"You have to admit, it makes sense. The media has reported there will be two of us there, but one makes just as much a target as two. We can fulfill the opportunity while minimizing our risks. Even you can see the sense in that."

What she could see was that Hawkins, the fed, was hanging behind them, pretending he wasn't interested in their low-pitched conversation. But she wasn't ready to let go of this yet. There was a burning stab of betrayal deep in her chest at his turnabout with the chief. She wondered for the first time if Dace was one of those officers who had difficulty working with women. She wouldn't have believed it, but his attitude now planted the seed of doubt. She'd met more than her share on the force who questioned a woman's ability to do the job with the same capability as a man.

Or else…he was trying to protect her. The thought had her throat drying out. The last time they'd made a decision based on his protective tendencies, devastation had followed.

"If this is your latent Galahad streak rearing its ugly head again, you need to bury it. Fast." She saw the change in his expression but refused to rein in her reaction. "On the job, I'm not a woman, I'm a cop. If you can't be objective about this, maybe you should bow out."

She'd wanted a response from him. She got it. He shoved his face close to hers. There was a glint of anger in his eyes, a lethal tone to his voice. "Is that what you want, Jolie? For me to be objective? You want a guy who will crawl into your bed at night and then stand by and watch you invite a bullet a couple days later?" He gave a grim nod. "Fine. You got it."

Turning on his heel, he walked away, fury apparent in every step. Aware that Hawkins was edging awkwardly in her direction, she followed in Dace's trail, more slowly. Dammit, he'd been out of line. She shouldn't be the one feeling small and petty for pointing it out to him. And throwing last night in her face had been an underhanded ploy.

It wasn't like she needed the reminder.

When she'd awakened this morning, still in that foggy state between sleep and wakefulness, she'd experienced a curious sense of déjà vu. For a moment she'd been transported back in time to when she used to share a bed with Dace.

Not at the end, when they'd each feigned sleep, hugging their sides of the bed, taking care not to touch each other. But before Sammy's funeral. Before even his birth. When the passion had flared, scorching and frequent. Until their relationship had gotten complicated beyond all measure.

An involuntary shudder worked through her. Last night had proven that the passion was still scorching. Dace had an effect on her that no other man could come close to matching. The admission was dismaying. But the complications from their fractured past still loomed, grim and insurmountable.

Dace was seated at the computer when she entered the room, tapping in a command. He didn't speak, and she was loath to break the brittle silence. She sat down at her post from yesterday, unenthusiastically pulling out the notes she'd taken on parolees with bank robbery convictions. Dace had given Dawson's file back to Truman that morning.

"I called that buddy of mine in OMPF/PERMS while you were in the shower this morning. We should be hearing from him later today." His voice was distant, impersonal. Jolie both welcomed that distance and knew what it said about her.

"So what are you working on now?"

"I've got responses from nine of the prisons in surrounding areas regarding the information requests we sent yesterday. We can start working from the notes we started."

"From the surveillance photos we saw last night, even taking the disguises into consideration, the HT's accomplice appears about ten years older than John."

"Let's focus first on parolees native to the western United States, ages thirty-eight to forty-five." Dace sounded as impersonal as if he were addressing a stranger. "Get me a copy of the list you make. I'll print out copies of the info from the prisons to cross-reference. We can see if anything pops while we're waiting to hear from Ben." At her questioning look, he elaborated tersely, "My buddy."

She gave a short nod and got to work. The feds would have gone down this road already, of course, although the records detailing the course of the investigation had been sparse in the files they'd seen. But they wouldn't have been looking for what she and Dace were. They wouldn't have been trying to link recent parolees with recently dismissed military with OPFOR training.

Jolie got to work, glad to have something to focus on. Anything that took even a portion of her attention away from Dace, and the impossible situation between them, was welcome distraction.

The task of cross-referencing names and information was tedious. They worked through lunch. When she glanced at her watch and saw it was approaching one o'clock, she rose. "I took a couple hours' medical leave this afternoon. I should be back by three."

Dace looked up from the pile of paperwork he was sifting through. "What's wrong?"

She hesitated, her innate need for privacy warring with a vague sense of guilt. She'd never been completely open with him, even from the first. And although she doubted it would have changed anything, perhaps she had owed him candidness, at least.

"My mother has a doctor's appointment. Hart will bring her, meeting me there. Hawkins will drive." She rose, getting her purse, extracting her sunglasses.

His silence made her nervous. She could still feel his eyes on her. "I better drop by the chief's office and let him know. I doubt the leave request made its way that far up the ladder."

To her dismay, Dace rose. "What the hell. I already pissed you off once today. I'm coming with you."

A dart of sheer panic pierced her chest, lodged there. Maybe she'd owed him an explanation about Trixie once upon a time, but that didn't mean she was ready to rectify her lapse by having them meet. Ever. "That isn't necessary. Hawkins can—"

"—take both of us as easily as just you." He rounded the table to approach her. "And if there's anything out of the ordinary, an extra pair of eyes isn't going to hurt."

He placed his hand at the small of her back, nudging her toward the door. She planted her feet and refused to budge, saying, "We've already done this today. You said…you *indicated* that you could be objective where it came to me on this case."

With his hand exerting more pressure, she was moved reluctantly toward the door. "I lied."

Dace realized Jolie must have discussed her intentions for today earlier with the feds, because when they entered the hallway they found Truman waiting with Hawkins. If either of the men thought it was odd that Dace was accompanying them, neither of them mentioned it.

He'd surprised even himself when the words left his mouth. But it was stupid for them to split up. Stupid to provide the subject with an extra opportunity to take one of them out. Yeah, they wore Kevlar vests beneath their clothes. The cars they rode in were inspected routinely for IEDs. But neither those measures nor the accompanying agents protected them from a head shot.

The smart thing to do would have been to insist Hart deliver Jolie's mother to the doctor himself. But he'd learned long ago to determine which battles weren't worth fighting. Instinctively, he knew this was one of them. Maybe the agents had discovered the same for themselves.

Conversation in the car was sparse. Truman wore a dour expression, but as it was his usual demeanor, it wasn't necessarily a reflection on his opinion of their outing.

He could tell when they were getting close to their destination by Jolie's increasing tension. Although behind her shades her eyes were unreadable, her spine seemed to grow stiffer with each passing mile. His gaze dropped to her lap. Her index finger was tapping a rapid tattoo on one leg in a rare display of nerves.

She wanted him to be objective. Hell, he could do objective. But that didn't keep him from wondering what had her so tense. Was it the upcoming appointment? Or the fact that he'd invited himself along?

Hawkins turned into the drive leading to the hospital. Bypassing the parking lot, he drove up to the front entrance to let them out beneath a canopy welcoming them to St. Michael's. Truman got out first, scanning the surrounding area carefully before gesturing for them to join him.

Once inside, Jolie took the lead, striding down a labyrinth of hallways and corridors. When she pushed open a set of double doors, Dace paused a moment to read the stenciled window. Oncology Center.

…she's dying of cancer. Other than that she's the same. Exactly the same.

Her words from the night before echoed, lingered. He

couldn't afford to dwell on them. It wasn't "objective" to wonder how the woman had happened back into Jolie's life. Or why the hell Jolie would bother with a woman who had abandoned her as a child.

When they reached a set of offices, Jolie paused, her hand on the doorknob, and looked back at them. "You can wait here. This shouldn't take more than twenty minutes."

Truman shrugged and she sent a quick glance in Dace's direction, he assumed to let him know that the order included him, too. So he hung back and let her enter alone. The fed leaned a shoulder against the wall, in a stance obviously meant for waiting. Dace positioned himself farther down the hall so that he could see into the waiting area of the office.

He saw Hart seated near a thin bleached-blonde who was flipping listlessly through a magazine. He stepped closer to the windows, curious in spite of himself. Other than her coloring and slight build, Jolie shared no real resemblance with her mother.

The young agent surged to his feet when he saw Jolie and took her aside. As Dace watched curiously, the conversation had the color leaching from Jolie's expression. She disengaged herself to approach her mother and it was clear from the sneer on the other woman's mouth, the way her lips twisted as she spoke, that the exchange was unpleasant.

He'd taken two steps to the door before he caught himself. Jolie could handle herself. He had no doubts of that. And it wasn't like she needed, or wanted, him to run interference. She wasn't his concern. Hadn't been for a long time.

Jamming his hands in his pockets, he caught Hart's gaze on him through the glass, nodded curtly. Then he forced himself to turn around and mimic Truman's stance against a wall, if some distance from the agent. The little drama unfolding in the doctor's office had nothing to do with him.

But he couldn't help but believe it would explain a hell of a lot about Jolie and what had shaped her into the woman she was today.

About ten minutes later, Hart exited the office and crossed over to him. "Conrad said Special Agent Truman was with you."

Dace jerked his head toward the other agent down the hall, and the younger man nodded. "I'm going to speak with him for a few minutes. Trixie just got called in so Conrad's back in the doctor's office with her. I have no idea how long it will take, but if you want to go inside and wait, we've got it covered out here."

"Trixie? That's Jolie's mother?"

Hart snorted. "She's a piece of work. I don't know what I did to deserve this detail. Actually caught her trying to sneak johns in her bedroom window last night, you believe that? The woman's a burnout. She'll do anything to get her hands on enough money to score a nickel bag." He started to shuffle in the other direction. "Come to think of it, I don't know what Conrad did to deserve the old hag. At least I'm rid of her after this case is over. She's stuck with her until the woman croaks. Which, at the rate she's going, won't take long."

Dace stood for a long moment, mulling over the agent's words as he stared blindly into the glass office windows across the hall. Whatever he had imagined of Jolie's past, it was obviously worse, much worse, than he'd thought. And Hart's careless words struck a chord.

Because it was obvious that Jolie had done nothing to deserve having a woman like Trixie as a mother. It was just as obvious that she'd never quite accepted that for herself.

It was close to a half hour before Jolie and her mother returned. And Dace heard them before he saw them.

"I don't give a damn what Baxter says. He don't run me

and neither do you. I got rights. I don't gotta do nothing I don't wanna do."

The two reentered the waiting area, an argument in progress. Jolie's voice was strained. "You heard him. The radiation treatments haven't halted the spread of the tumor. Chemo is the next logical option."

"Logical." Trixie snorted. "Ain't nothing logical about nuking me to death. I ain't going through all that, losing my hair, looking like a freak when I'm gonna die anyway."

Jolie winced a little, and shushed the other woman, shooting a quick look at the dozen or so occupants of the room. It was only then that her gaze landed on Dace. "We can talk about it later."

"Already told you both. Ain't nothing to talk about." The older woman began to rummage in her bag, taking out a pack of cigarettes.

"You're not lighting that in here."

Dace rose lazily to his feet as they approached, heard the steel in Jolie's tone.

"Like I say, you don't run me."

He reached out and plucked the package from the woman's fingers. "Why don't I hold these until you get outside the hospital."

The woman shot him a narrowed look, and he stemmed her protest by sticking out his hand. "We haven't met. I'm Dace Recker. Jolie and I—"

Trixie interrupted him as his hand engulfed hers. "I know who you are."

"Ms. Conrad?"

Jolie didn't look eager to leave them alone, but the receptionist was growing impatient. "I have to schedule the next appointment," she said in low tones. "Keep your voices down and watch your wallet."

Dace lifted a surprised brow, but she moved away. He shifted his attention to Trixie, noting the older woman's appraising stare.

"So you're the one knocked her up. Hope you got smarter since then. The last thing she needs is to get stuck with another kid."

The verbal blow, delivered in that caustic tone, hit its mark. He assessed her with new caution. Despite the too-youthful, figure-hugging short skirt and halter top, Trixie looked prematurely old. Her eyes were sunken, her face deeply wrinkled, and she was missing several teeth. The long bottle-blond hair was thinning.

The signs were glaring. Trixie was an addict. From the devastation done her appearance, he'd guess meth head. And he doubted she'd given it up willingly.

The woman looked him up and down, a flicker of appreciation in her expression. "Well, easy enough to see why she decided to take you for a ride. But seems to me you owe her for putting her through all that. Losing a kid…that's a hard thing for a woman. I should know. Damn social services yanked Jolie away from me without any cause or warning." She paused, as if waiting for a word of sympathy, before going on. "She'd never ask for herself, but I'm guessing you can afford to throw her a little money. Go a long way toward making up for getting her pregnant to begin with."

His throat tightened. One fist curled, before he remembered he still held her cigarettes in it. "You think I should pay Jolie off for having Sammy?"

"That his name?" Trixie threw a quick glance over her shoulder. Jolie was still busy with the receptionist. She returned her attention to Dace, speaking more hurriedly. "Wouldn't have to be a lot. Maybe ten thousand or so. She wouldn't take it. Got her pride from me. But I'd keep it for her. Help out with the expenses, rent and food. All the damn pills they keep shoving on me. You do the right thing here, you'd be helping her out, whether she knows it or not."

"An interesting proposition."

"What is?" Jolie strode up to them where they stood engaged in conversation, looking from one of them to the other. Her gaze narrowed. "Trixie? What'd you say now?"

The skinny woman shook her hair back in a gesture that looked more pathetic than haughty. "Just saying wouldn't kill him to cough up some dough. Make up some for you going through what you did. Having that kid die and all." When Jolie's expression went murderous, the other woman's voice turned to a whine. "Don't get all pissy. I was just thinking of you. He owes you. Maybe you can't see that, but I can."

"Too bad you had no idea who my father was. You could have performed this little shakedown on your own behalf."

Dace had often damned Jolie's ability to shut down, to keep an expressionless mask during emotional turmoil. But he'd never heard the cold tone she used now.

"Yeah, too bad." Trixie grabbed for her cigarettes, real regret lacing her words. "I could have had me a time with money like that."

She sauntered toward the door, leaving Dace and Jolie frozen behind her. Because he was watching closely, Dace could see the effort it took for Jolie to recover her impassive mask, as if she were rebuilding her defenses one stone at a time.

Her expression was blank, but she couldn't hide the terrible bleakness in her eyes. "Like I said," she remarked as she followed her mother to the door, "she's no June Cleaver."

Chapter 11

"Why don't you check your e-mail. See if your friend has gotten back to you."

They'd barely reentered their assigned quarters at the administration building before Jolie issued the suggestion. Dace studied her for a moment, but every sign of vulnerability had been firmly bricked away.

She'd had ample time to recover her poise during the car ride back to police admin. She'd engaged Truman in a conversation regarding the security at Soldier's Square, the park where the memorial was to be held the following day. And even Dace had found himself distracted by talk of K-9 units, countersnipers, full perimeter security forces and protective positioning on the dais tomorrow. Only two entrances would be open and access would be controlled by busing the general public and media in.

But now they were alone, and he had to consider whether

to let her use the case to regain a professional footing or take the opportunity to pry out even more information about her past.

He had no problem hitting a guy when he was down, if it would get him the information he wanted. But somehow he couldn't bring himself to use the events of the past couple hours to leverage more personal details from her.

Realizing that pissed him off. He was going soft. No doubt about it. He'd promised himself just last night that he was going to take every opportunity to learn more about what made Jolie Conrad tick. Because she didn't share willingly, he was going to grab any chance he could to force the answers from her if he had to.

But he really no longer needed to. Brushing by her, he crossed to the laptop he'd been using and brought up his e-mail account. That brief encounter with Trixie had connected enough dots that he could complete the picture for himself. It also made it easier to understand where Jolie's distrust regarding family came from. And a whole lot harder to blame her for those defenses that were so much a part of her.

If Trixie had been his mother, he wouldn't just have defenses, he'd have constructed a goddamn fortress.

So he let her set the tone and shifted his focus to the investigation. If he were honest with himself, he didn't really want to see her eyes go desolate again. Didn't want to see the hint of vulnerability that had flickered before she regained control. She deserved a freaking break, a chance to recover. He was going to give her that much. If that meant he wasn't being objective, well, she'd never know the difference, would she?

He felt a spark of adrenaline when he sat down at the computer and saw an e-mail from Ben. The subject header read: You owe me. "It's here."

Jolie came to stand behind him, reading over his shoulder

as he brought up the e-mail. Ben had grandiose ideas about what his help was worth, as usual, and it was accompanied with the usual good-natured insults traded between Marines of Charlie and Bravo companies. But as Dace downloaded the accompanying attachment, he had to admit that if the info panned out the way they hoped, he'd be inclined to think of a fitting thank-you for his buddy. Hopefully one that wouldn't cost him a month's paycheck.

He wasn't big on having people reading over his shoulder, but this time he welcomed another pair of eyes. "Any of these names sound familiar?"

"Let me get that list I made."

He typed in a command to print a copy of the attachment and then returned to the document to read further. There were a lot of names, but they'd be cross-referencing surnames with those on the parolee list. And if that didn't yield a hit, they'd look at the records they'd gotten from the visitor logs and next of kin from the prisons.

"Did you make me a—" A copy of the parolee list was jammed into his hand a moment before Jolie crossed again to the printer to collect the downloaded pages from OMPF/PERMS. She returned with the pages and pulled out a chair next to him, spreading the papers out before her.

It was a daunting task. Ben's list was arranged alphabetically rather than in order of date of release from military service. "The robberies started several months ago. Let's concentrate on the military releases in the past two years who had OPFOR or Special Forces duties. You take the first ten pages of names, I'll take the next ten."

His lips twitched. She was methodical in organization, whether it came to the lists she made or the way she approached a task. It came, he supposed, from having no control in the first years of her life.

He put the sheaf of papers aside and turned his attention to the computer screen. "Okay, shoot."

"Abel."

They worked in near silence for almost three hours. When they came to *Jones* the work slowed to a crawl as they cross-checked the common surname between the two lists and the prison records. Dace hated to think of how long it was going to take them to get through the Smiths.

As it turned out, they didn't have to find out. Jolie reached out, grabbed his arm. "Marker, Adam Kevin. Take a look." He leaned over to read from the paper she was holding out for him, rather than trying to find the copy in his own pile. "Paroled twenty-two months ago from NSP-Nevada, where he did a fifteen-year stint for armed bank robbery. Born in Santa Monica forty years ago."

"Right age," Dace muttered, reaching for the next page she produced. This one was from OMPF/PERMS. "David John Marker." He exchanged a grim look with Jolie. The HT had asked to be called John. "No Special Forces history but long stints on OPFOR units, first in Afghanistan, then Baghdad. Released thirteen months ago. Born…" He frowned. "In Utah? Thirty years ago."

He grabbed the sheaf of material they'd requested from the prison systems. "Did we get a response from NSP?" He began riffling through them.

"They're in alphabetical order."

He shot her a look. "Of course they are." None of the Jones matches had panned out, but Marker wasn't as common a name.

"Well, we know now they aren't father and son," Jolie said. "But they could be brothers. Maybe half brothers, to explain the difference in ages."

Pulling out the NSP sheet, Dace put it on the table between

them, running his finger down the list of names until he found Marker. Fifteen years was a long time but the list of visitors was remarkably short. Either the man hadn't had much family, friends or both.

But one name appeared on the list on an almost yearly basis.

Marker. David, John.

"You called it, half brothers." Dace sat back in his chair, a little surprised they'd actually found a connection. "Earlier in the sentence David showed up a couple times a year. That slows down about the time he joined the Army. Every twelve or fourteen months. Which would have correlated with his leave."

"The feds would have tracked the parolee angle first thing." Reservation sounded in Jolie's voice. "If this is our guy, why didn't he pop for them when they were following up on the lead?"

Dace shook his head. "He covered himself somehow. I don't know. We can't be sure this is our link until we get them to run a DNA match on the HT from the blood at the scene with the samples military personnel give. And that isn't a database we can access."

"So we give it to the chief. The FBI's antiterrorism unit and Homeland Security are connected to this case. There isn't a government database in existence that DHS can't get to."

"We just have to convince Sanders the connection is solid."

Jolie glanced at her watch, then stood, began collecting the papers they'd been working with and putting them in order. "And then he has to convince the feds. It's a quarter to five. He wanted to see us at the end of the day anyway. Let's give him what we have and we can go over the rest of the list at home tonight."

His stomach clutched. *Home.* Once they'd had a home together, but he didn't read anything into the word the way she used it now. He finally understood just how unlikely a pair they had made three years ago. He who had considered a home and family as a natural course of things. And she, to whom both must have seemed alien.

He rose when she did, following her to the door. It was humbling to admit that she'd nailed him dead to rights with the accusation she'd leveled at him earlier. He was no one's idea of a white knight—she was dead wrong on that—but protective, yeah. Hard to deny it. Today marked the second time he'd tried to get her taken off this detail and gotten his ass chewed because of it.

It was damn ironic that he still felt compelled to shield her from physical danger. Especially since he was beginning to understand that no physical harm could rival the emotional damage inflicted by her childhood.

"So, let me get this straight." Sanders rubbed his jaw with one pawlike hand. "You're saying knowledge of incendiary devices similar to the ones used on Conrad's car and at the bank site could have been acquired in the military. And you've got a guy with that expertise recently released from service, who is a half brother to a paroled bank robber."

"That's right, sir." Jolie took the lead in the conversation, more than a little surprised that Dace let her. If he were sitting there contemplating how he could get her off this assignment again, she'd be better prepared this time. Dealing with Trixie gave her a lot of hands-on experience counteracting manipulation.

"To eliminate David Marker as a suspect," she continued, "we'd need a test run comparing his DNA—which was taken from the blood left at the site—to his DNA sample in the military databases. With the high level of federal involvement on this case, it shouldn't be difficult."

"Problem is, Fenholt seems pretty damn certain their information regarding activities of a terrorist sleeper cell is accurate." Sanders surveyed them both from beneath lowered brows. "I'm sure they've been over the recent parolees with a fine-tooth comb. They'd have nailed this Marker if he were the least bit suspicious."

"Maybe that means he's smart enough not to arouse suspicion," Dace put in. "We're the ones who talked to the HT. There was no hint of any terrorist leanings. No clue of disenfranchisement with this government or its policies. Trouble with authority, sure. If we accessed his full military personnel file, I'm willing to bet we'll find plenty of references to insubordination, or worse. But he told us himself, he was in the bank because that's where the money was."

"And you think it's as simple as that?"

"We both do."

Sanders drummed his blunt-edged fingers on the desktop. "Well, it's worth checking out. I'll try to push them to get it done quickly. Is that the only connection you've made between the ex-military and parolees?"

"It's the first so far, and we're halfway through the list," Jolie responded. "We'll finish it tonight and let you know if we find anything else."

"Do that." A change in his expression heralded a shift of topic. "I had a long meeting with SAC Fenholt and some of her unit. They seem to agree with you that your appearance tomorrow is vital if they hope to draw the subject out."

Jolie had to school herself not to glance in Dace's direction. But she could feel her heart thudding in her chest in anticipation of the chief's decision.

Folding his arms on his desk, he leaned forward, lowered

his voice. "No one in this department would blame either of you for sitting this one out. What they're asking of you... well, it's a risk some wouldn't feel worth taking. I'm giving you both an opportunity to stand down. No questions asked. No consequences. Think it over carefully, because it's your last chance."

"My mind hasn't changed since I volunteered for this, sir," Jolie said firmly. The only difference between her first agreement and now was the mounting body count. "He has to be stopped. I'm willing to do my part."

"I'm going to be there, too." Dace's voice was inflexible.

The chief nodded. Jolie couldn't tell if he was relieved or disappointed. "I've arranged some further security for you. You'll arrive in a department-issued armored vehicle. A three-sided canopy over the dais will limit positioning of a sniper." Despite herself, Jolie felt a shiver crawl down her spine. "Of course, K-9 units will be in continuous use and a full police presence will be maintained. If something goes down, for God's sake, don't try to be heroes. Get the hell out of there. Once you leave, bystanders will be a whole lot safer."

Mingled relief and anticipation worked over her. The detail would go forward and maybe, if they got real lucky, this case would be broken by this time tomorrow.

If they got even luckier, she and Dace would live through it.

Saturday dawned with clear skies and projected temperatures in the mid-seventies. The memorial service was scheduled for 10:00 a.m. Because of the difficulty getting the armored vehicle through a large crowd and close to the stage, Dace and Jolie would arrive two hours early, but remain in the vehicle until starting time.

Like any well-laid plan, it was destined to fail.

The first hint of trouble came when a tap sounded on

Jolie's bedroom door shortly after dawn. Sleep had been elusive. She'd lain there for hours before dozing off, and then wakened just a few hours later.

She refused to believe that sleeping alone had anything to do with that.

Last night she and Dace had worked until after midnight, but had found no other connection similar to that of the Marker brothers. Regardless of the feds' terrorist link, she shared Dace's confidence that the half brothers were a solid lead. She only hoped it was treated with the urgency from the Bureau that it deserved.

Jolie opened the door to see Dawson and Dace standing in the hallway. Neither had shaved. Dace was bare-chested, while Dawson had a half-buttoned shirt on. But it was the agent's bare feet that startled her the most. She'd never seen him any less than meticulously dressed.

Foreboding pooled in the pit of her stomach.

"What's wrong?"

"I need both of you to come downstairs." The fed was already moving toward the steps, so Jolie cocked a brow at Dace. He lifted a shoulder. Whatever it was, the agent hadn't seen fit to tell him either.

Since she was decently dressed in an old tee and pajama shorts, she padded down the stairs behind Dace. It occurred to her that had she not elected to sleep in the spare bedroom last night, the fed would have found her in Dace's bed, where she'd slept Thursday night.

When they got downstairs Dawson was seated at the kitchen counter. Dace and Jolie took a chair on either side of him. Habit had Jolie looking in the direction of the automatic coffeemaker. She had a feeling she was going to need the fortification.

"I don't want to alarm you," the agent began.

Too late, Jolie thought. Nerves were already jumping and quivering in her stomach.

"But you deserve to be kept abreast of the most recent developments in the security detail for today."

"Just spit it out," Dace muttered. He wasn't, Jolie recalled, much of a morning person. For that matter, neither was she.

Dawson looked at each of them in turn, his expression sober. "As you know, security has been tight at the memorial location. Top-level scrutiny. Special Agent in Charge Fenholt and Special Agent Pedersen, from the antiterrorism unit, walked it yesterday evening. But a couple hours ago the K-9 units were brought back to the site to do another thorough sweep and then to remain throughout the ceremony." He drew a breath. "The dogs are responding to dozens of spots throughout the inside perimeter."

"Dozens?" Jolie was stunned. "Dozens of bombs?" Was that possible? Dace had guessed that David Marker had been the explosives expert. But he could have taught his brother what he knew before he died.

"There haven't been any explosives discovered."

Somehow Jolie didn't find Dawson's declaration particularly reassuring. Either the explosives were so well hidden they wouldn't be found until too late, or the K-9 units were failing in their task.

"Someone got in there," Dace said flatly. "Scattered a scent—probably gunpowder—at various points to distract the dogs, divert the handlers and the bomb squad. And there wouldn't be much purpose in distraction if there weren't an IED planted on the premises. At least one."

Jolie could see from the agent's expression that he'd arrived at the same conclusion.

"We've got an ATF bomb squad in place in addition to your local unit. You can be assured that public access will be limited until we're certain the site is safe."

Dace stood and without a word strode for the stairs. Jolie frowned at his abrupt departure, but her mind was on the information the agent had just imparted.

"So there was a breach sometime between the time those dogs left yesterday and this morning. Not exactly comforting."

Dawson had the grace to look ill at ease. "It would appear so. I haven't been to the site myself in the past twenty-four hours. But the security plans were painstaking. I don't see how a breach could occur. But no plan is infallible."

Silently, Jolie agreed. Any strategy was only as good as the people implementing it. All it took was one distraction. One guy out of position. And a patient outsider would have the opportunity he sought.

Dace was jogging back down the steps. Jolie recognized the blown-up picture he clutched in his hand. He crossed to Dawson and laid it down in front of him. "I think you need to make copies of this and hand it out to the security detail at the scene."

The agent picked it up to study more closely. "Markham, right? Why do you have a picture of him?"

"Adam Marker," Dace corrected. "And we think it's possible that this is the guy we're looking for."

"Marker. That's it." Dawson set the picture down and shook his head. "I don't know what makes you suspect him, but I can tell you he's not our guy. I checked him out myself, shortly after the first robbery."

"How can you be so sure it's not him?"

Before answering Dace's question, the man got up and went to the coffeemaker, poured three mugs of coffee, then delivered one to Jolie. He picked up the other two containers and set one in front of Dace, retaining the other.

"He had an alibi for all but one of the robberies," he replied finally. "He was at work. Learned automotive repair at NSP and has been steadily employed for a small auto-repair business in Bakersfield since shortly after he was paroled. I've talked to his boss. Seen his time cards. He checks out."

Disappointment blooming, Jolie wrapped her hands around the steaming mug and lifted it to sip. Okay, they knew the feds would have followed up on the recent parolees. But the link they'd found between the Marker brothers had seemed so promising. "Any chance his alibi is phony? Maybe bought and paid for?"

Dawson lifted a shoulder, the gesture curiously casual for a man usually so proper. "Anything's possible. Just like it's possible that Joseph Welch's medical records showing he isn't ambulatory could be phony. Or that Jeremy Saul wasn't at his grandmother's bedside for a month prior to her death, during three of the robberies. Anything's possible. But probable? No."

Jolie recognized the names of the men he mentioned as others on the list of recent parolees. "You really believe members of a sleeper cell are responsible."

"Those details are classified." The man drank, his eyes sliding shut in appreciation of the strong brew. "But trust me. They are convincing."

A cell phone rang, and immediately Jolie looked around for her purse. Since she wasn't living with Trixie at the moment, she didn't feel the need to lock it up each night. Not that she had a car to lock it in anymore.

But it wasn't her phone or Dace's. Agent Dawson walked by them and picked up his cell from the coffee table next to the couch. She listened unabashedly but could tell nothing from his side of the conversation.

Feeling Dace's gaze on her, Jolie lifted her eyes to meet his, reading his thoughts with an ease that frightened her. He wasn't ready to give up on the Marker lead. Neither was she. But they had more important things to worry about for the next few hours.

Dawson snapped the receiver of his cell closed, looking a bit rattled. He recovered almost immediately, smoothing his expression to a reassuring mask. "They've found an explosive. ATF is containing it as we speak. The rest of the units will continue to follow up on all of the dogs' alerts, but I'm willing to bet you were right." He nodded at Dace. "The distraction was all about calling our attention away from the bomb."

Her skin prickled. "Where'd they find it?"

At first Jolie didn't think Dawson was going to answer. His gaze slid past hers. "It was attached to the plywood skirting below the dais."

Nine fifty-seven a.m. Two minutes later than the last time Jolie had checked her watch. Time had crawled to a stop since the armored vehicle had halted next to the stage, fifteen minutes ago.

The past few hours had been spent in a state of uncertainty. Sanders had refused to allow the memorial to go forward until all alerts had been thoroughly checked out. Dace and she had paced his town house, not knowing whether their mission that day would be aborted or not. They hadn't been given the word that the assignment would go forward until forty-five minutes ago.

The park was bustling with activity. Jolie estimated there were well over a thousand people, not counting the wall of blue uniformed officers who'd come to pay their respects. She knew there would be even more law enforcement in plain clothes. It seemed improbable that the subject would appear, risking detection in such a heavily guarded arena.

But he'd successfully infiltrated the security once. Jolie was well aware that a motivated subject could do so again.

There was little doubt this subject was motivated.

Misgivings circled in her mind like busy little ants. What if the discovered explosive had been a decoy? What if another was still waiting out there somewhere, ready to detonate when the stage was occupied?

She scanned the area. The dais was the logical site for an explosive, with her and Dace as the targets. But if the subject didn't mind mass carnage, he could have planted a larger one farther away. Maybe on that statue of a Civil War soldier astride a horse. Or several hundred meters farther, in the fountain that spouted water in the air like a trio of belugas. There were several locations that could secret an IED. They'd have to trust that the dogs had done their job. That the distracting scent hadn't confused them.

Another glance at her watch. A minute had ticked by. Several men were unfurling a canopy atop the stage. Jolie watched with approval. The edge was trimmed with triangular pennants that would snap and move in the breeze even now causing the American flags to flap from flagpoles around the park. If the subject was out there with a rifle, the pennants would be a diversion. He'd also be forced to adjust for the wind.

She clasped her hands together, cracked her knuckles. And sitting here doing nothing was going to make her a raving paranoid before they even got to the stage.

"What's the holdup?" she muttered to Dace. "Where'd Truman and Dawson go?"

He turned from the opposite window. If he was suffering from any nerves, it didn't show. "These things never begin on time. Too many bureaucracies to coordinate." He studied her, probably seeing more in her expression than she would have liked. "It's a zoo out there. The subject isn't likely to know that the explosive has been discovered."

Meaning, of course, that he probably wouldn't be here to follow up with a sniper shot. It wasn't that Jolie didn't appreciate Dace's attempt to reassure her. She'd been a negotiator long enough to be well versed in human psychology. The truth was, the only predictable thing about this subject was his single-minded motivation to avenge the HT's death.

"Do me a favor and stay alert anyway, all right?" The words slipped past her guard without her conscious permission.

Dace's green eyes darkened. "I suppose it's useless to suggest you stay in the vehicle for the duration?"

That shot her spine with steel. "Useless *and* offensive."

He nodded. "I figured. So I won't say anything." Before she had a clue to his intentions, he leaned over, cupped her nape in his palm and covered her mouth with his.

Pent-up emotion poured into the kiss. Jolie could sense his frustration and something else. Something that might have been fear for her safety. His desire to shield her didn't annoy her as much as usual. She happened to be just as scared for him. And remorseful that he'd gotten into this thing because of her.

His tongue swept into her mouth, staking a claim. She didn't need comforting arms or encouraging words. She needed this unvarnished demand she could meet with her own. A quick hot pressure that reminded her of everything between them, past and present. And diverted her attention nicely from what might be out there waiting for them.

There was a rap at the window, and their lips parted even as the door was pulled open.

"Final security sweep has been executed. We're going to start." Truman ducked his head into the vehicle. "You two ready?"

With effort, Jolie tore her gaze away from Dace's. "More than." She reached for her sunglasses, placed them on her nose.

"Then let's do this."

She slid across the backseat and out the open door. Immediately, she was flanked by Truman and Dawson. When Dace joined them a moment later, two agents Jolie hadn't seen before came to stand next to him, one on each side. Each of them moved toward the stage in tandem with their security.

Jolie's glance encompassed the crowd and beyond. The sea of people stretched endlessly. A center aisle had been left in front of the stage.

She climbed the steps, one agent in back of her, one in front. Half a dozen people were already waiting there. Chief Sanders, resplendent in his dress uniform. Deputy Chief Grey. Mayor Owens, a woman whose policies Jolie had never much cared for. A couple councilmen. SAC Fenholt.

They filed to the far end of the stage and stopped. Jolie noted large framed posters atop stands scattered across the front of the stage. She knew without seeing the front of them that each would depict a likeness of one of the fallen officers. She doubted anyone in the crowd would realize the pictures served as yet another impediment to a sniper trying to get a clear shot.

Below, next to the center steps, was a table. Eight folded flags, each with a single white rose, sat atop it. The reminder of the officers' deaths solidified her sense of purpose. Regardless of the outcome, if there was a chance her appearance here today could bring their killer to justice, it was a risk worth taking. There was a familiar humming in her veins as Chief Sanders went to the microphone and began to speak. Adrenaline did a crazy little tap dance along her nerve endings as she turned her gaze to the mass of people before her.

Sanders spoke eloquently of the officers' sense of duty. Their selfless sacrifice in the face of danger. Jolie felt Truman stiffen on the other side of her, heard him murmuring something in the discreet mike he wore attached to his earpiece via a thin cord. She saw what had alerted him. There was a disturbance in the crowd after Sanders called up the first officer's widow. The agents on either side of her stepped forward, closing ranks, effectively shutting her from view.

It was another moment before they stepped back again. She saw that a member of the press, jockeying for a photo as Sanders walked down the front steps to the stage to meet the widow and hand her the flag and commemorative rose, had caused the disturbance.

Jolie released a breath she hadn't realized she'd been holding. Chief Deputy Grey announced the second officer's name. There was a glint of something in the distance, beyond the fountains. It was ridiculous to wonder if it were the sun bouncing off a rifle barrel. A shooter would be positioned in a tree. In the heavy shrubbery surrounding the park. The most accomplished sniper might be accurate from up to a mile away. But the subject hadn't tried shots at that distance. She was willing to bet any attempt would come from no more than five hundred yards.

With the plentiful vegetation, there would be no shortage of hiding places.

She shifted her attention to the women coming one by one up to accept their flag and flower. One woman walked slowly, her figure heavy with child, and the sight hurtled Jolie back in time. The changes in her body brought on by pregnancy had been foreign. More than a little frightening. How much more terrifying it would be for this woman, knowing that the child she would bear would never know his father.

She could feel a thin trickle of perspiration crawling from

her nape down her spine. The air was mild, but the bulky level-III vest with ceramic plates she wore beneath her ill-fitting oversize shirt increased her body temperature. Each time a camera flashed, she could see the agents beside her tense. But her attention remained on the unknown woman. She wondered how she planned to cope with the tragic events that had made her a single parent.

Odd, given her and Dace's occupations, but she had never once considered the possibility of having to raise Sammy on her own. A cop couldn't think about the risks on the job every day and still be effective. If she'd given it any thought at all, she had no doubt it would have terrified her enough that Dace would never have managed to persuade her to go through with the pregnancy.

She'd been alarmed enough over the situation as it was.

The podium mike gave a loud screech of feedback. Jolie jerked, nearly diving to the floor in response. Her heart jack-hammered in her chest. With grim effort, she willed her pulse to quiet. Another officer's name had been announced, Laeten's. The couple making their way up the center aisle was slight. Frail. Laeten's parents. Jolie seemed to recall hearing that the man had divorced years ago.

She'd lost track of time. How many names had been called? How many folded American flags handed to grieving relatives? Her gaze dropped to the table set up in front of the dais. Two flags left.

The perspiration was a pool at the base of her spine now. The body armor she wore weighed almost four pounds. The loose-fitting shirt she'd had to wear over it was unseasonably heavy. And the slight breeze stirring the leaves on the park's trees wasn't reaching the semi-enclosed stage.

The sound of a motor split the air. Jolie craned her neck to see a motorcycle speeding through the far end of the park.

She looked at Dace. With only two entrances in and out of the area, how the heck had the rider gotten through the outer perimeter?

She wasn't given an opportunity to examine the question. The federal agents nudged her to get her moving across the stage. With a start, Jolie realized the service was over. The entrance of the motorcycle, now nearly three-quarters of the way across the park, had drowned other sounds out.

Dawson was the first down the dais steps. Jolie followed, still distracted by the scene playing out across the park. Several plain-clothed officers were moving toward the motorcyclist. The driver revved the motor, increasing speed. Jolie had descended the first two steps when she felt a sting on her leg and looked down, stunned to see a large, jagged piece of wood distending from her pants leg.

"Get down! Get down!"

A heavy weight knocked her off her feet, and she tumbled down the remaining stairs. She heard screams. The sound of the motor, farther away this time. And the crack of a second shot.

Jolie hit the ground with enough force to drive the breath from her lungs. Someone—Dawson? Truman?—pinned her to the ground.

But the arm next to her face wasn't clothed in a dark suit coat. It was enclosed in a blue shirtsleeve. It wasn't an agent on top of her, it was Dace. And there was blood spattered on the fabric. A small pool forming on the ground next to her hand.

Chapter 12

"You're an idiot."

After the blunt pronouncement, Jolie stalked toward the apartment, her back rigid. Dace slammed the door of the armored car with his good arm, wincing a little as the effort pulled at his patched shoulder.

Dawson slid him a sidelong glance as they followed the steamed woman toward the front door. "Only fools ignore the advice of their doctors or lawyers."

"I don't like hospitals." And Jolie, of all people, had no room to talk about following doctor's orders. He'd been unwise enough to point that out, eliciting the earlier comment and a few others much less polite. "It's a flesh wound. It won't heal any faster if I lie in a hospital bed another twenty-four hours."

Truman opened the door as they headed up the front steps. Jolie swept inside. She was as ticked as Dace had ever seen her, and he couldn't quite figure why. Adrenaline letdown, maybe. They'd been hustled into the armored vehicle with such speed that it had been impossible to see what was going on with the shooter. They'd had to rely on updates from the agents, and the news hadn't been good. The subject had gotten away on the back of the motorcycle that had provided the diversion. It had been found abandoned less than ten miles away.

The bastard always seemed to be one step ahead of them. If that was what had Jolie out of sorts, he could sympathize. He felt the same way.

"So what's next?" Jolie was asking Truman as Dace walked in. "The memorial drew the shooter out, just the way Fenholt wanted. Does she have a fallback plan now that the subject managed to slip through the fingers of two departments?"

"Options are being discussed. We're supposed to leave immediately for a debriefing downtown."

Truman's tone was terse. Dace could tell he didn't like being reminded just how badly the Bureau had screwed up. Jesus. He shook his head in disbelief. The dirtbag managed to get an explosive on the site and park himself close enough to get a couple shots off. And then got clean away, which was really the pisser. If he was going to take a bullet, the least the feds could do was make the damn arrest.

He wondered if Fenholt was across town with the other feebies trying to figure out a way to blame this on the locals, which would be totally bogus. The Bureau had called the shots all the way. And maybe that was the problem.

Truman and Dawson stepped aside, discussing something in low tones. Dace's attention, however, was on Jolie. She walked straight through the family room, heading for the stairs. He didn't want to think about the ice-cold blade of fear that had stabbed through him when he'd heard that first shot. Seen how close it had come to her.

His lungs clogged at the memory. Time had frozen into still frames. The bullet creasing the wood steps. The ugly thick splinter lodged in Jolie's leg. Shoving the agent aside and diving for Jolie. Panic sprinting through his veins. Afraid of a second shot. Afraid he'd be too late.

He hadn't even been aware he'd been hit until he'd seen the blood on his shirt. For one awful moment, he'd thought it was Jolie's.

When Truman spoke, it took Dace a moment to realize the words were meant for him. "The rifle used in the shooting was left behind. It's been dusted for prints, but it had been wiped clean."

Of course it would be. Dace's mouth flattened. They were due, way overdue, for a break in this case.

The agent continued. "There was a visual of the shooter as he was driving away, at least from the back. He was wearing a SWAT Tac-Vest."

Dace stared at him, the words coming as if from a distance. An LEO was responsible? Was it possible?

Everything inside him rejected the idea. But doubts filtered in and wouldn't be banished. It would explain how the subject had infiltrated security. Maybe he had an ID. It didn't necessarily mean he was LEO, only that he'd accessed law enforcement equipment.

And yet…someone had leaked the names of the SWAT personnel on-site at the bank. Admin had been leaning heavily on the dispatchers and reporters with the police beat. Maybe they should have been looking closer to home.

But it was one thing to think it. It was another to hear Truman practically repeat his thoughts a moment later. "Looks like you guys might need to look in-house. Local departments are notorious for corruption."

Dace's fingers curled into a fist. "Screw you, Truman.

Anyone with access to the Internet can get police-issue vests.
For that matter, it could just as easily be someone with a connection to the feds."

"It's extremely doubtful either way," Agent Dawson put
in. "He wore what he needed to blend in. He's adaptable,
and the panic in the crowd made it impossible to mount a
quick pursuit. The good news is that one of our snipers got
a shot off and is sure he hit the rider on the back. Probably
the shooter."

"If he was wearing a vest, a bullet didn't do more than stun
him," Dace said flatly. The pain reliever they'd pressed on him
at the hospital was starting to wear off. His arm was beginning
to throb. Diplomacy be damned. The events of the day were
combining to knock him on his ass. "I wouldn't pin my hopes
on that. These guys are making you look like a bunch of
mutts."

He started for the steps. "I'm going to take a shower. I'll
be ready to go in a few minutes."

He'd only gone a few steps when Truman said, "Your
presence isn't required downtown. It's an agency session."

The words halted him in midstep. Turning to face the two
men, he saw the truth in their expressions. "Yeah. I'll bet it
is." He studied them for another moment. "Is Fenholt pulling
the detail off us?"

"That hasn't been determined," Agent Dawson put in. He
started for the door. "We'll leave the two men outside until
further notice."

He waited as the pair walked through the door, then locked
it after them. The turn of events wasn't totally surprising. But
for the first time he considered just what their options would
be if the feds decided on a whole new game plan. Would they
be expected to join the other SWAT members on leave? He
doubted the city could afford that option much longer.

He hesitated on his way to the bathroom and looked in on Jolie. She'd switched the bulky shirt and armor for a tee the same shade as her eyes. She'd never leave the city willingly. Her mother's health tied her here. She was seated at the desk in the spare bedroom, the contents of the case file spread before her. But she didn't look like her mind was on it. The pencil she was holding beat a rapid tattoo against the pile of paper.

He eyed her uncertainly. Since he'd never seen her in this mood before, he had no idea how to defuse it. In the end, he seized on the investigation. That, at least, was a neutral topic. "The blame game already is starting downtown. Truman and Dawson just left for their seats at the table." He relayed Truman's speculation about the subject's possible background, finishing, "Hell, if he was law enforcement, he'd be a helluva lot better shot."

Her jaw tightened, and she bent over the papers, pencil in hand. "Well, he was nearly good enough, wasn't he?"

It didn't take a rocket scientist to interpret that caustic tone. He had three sisters. He knew when he was in dangerous territory. Dace backed out of the room. "I'm gonna take a shower." Stating his intent almost made him feel like he wasn't running. Almost.

When he got to the bathroom he rummaged through the medicine chest for a pain reliever. He wasn't going to take the pain meds the hospital had sent home. Damn pills slowed his thinking.

As he swallowed some ibuprofen, he noticed that Jolie had already stacked extra dressings and gauze on the counter. Padding over to the shower, he reached in and turned on the water. All he wanted to do was let the showerhead pound out the stress of the day.

As he took off his shirt, the bathroom door pushed open

behind him. "Are you counting on your superpowers to keep the dressing dry?"

Guiltily he glanced down at his arm. "I was planning to wrap a towel around it," he lied. Probably not a good time to tell her he figured she could change the dressing for him. Or he could do it himself. Probably.

Her mouth a grim line, she marched to the counter and snatched up the plastic bag the materials had come in. He couldn't make out the words she was muttering under her breath. Probably just as well.

With a few swift movements she had the bag wrapped around his dressing and secured with a couple of rubber bands, her touch decidedly ungentle.

"Thanks." He eased away. "Good thing you're a cop. Your bedside manner could use some work."

As a joke, it failed miserably. She stared at him, something alight in her eyes that he couldn't identify. A moment later it turned to temper, and that, unfortunately, was all too easy to recognize. "I was wrong earlier," she snapped. "You aren't an idiot. You're a complete moron." She turned and slammed from the room, leaving him to stare dumbly after her.

Christ. What had just happened? He didn't remember ever getting this attitude from her before, and frankly, it was starting to piss him off.

He stripped off the rest of his clothes, pulled open the shower door and stepped inside. Bracing his hand against the shower wall, he lifted his face to the spray and let out a deep breath. Hell, he thought aggrievedly. If she was frustrated with the screwup at the park, he'd been there, too. They weren't going to get any closer to solving this case by spending their time at each other's throats.

A moment later the door was yanked open, and he swiped the water from his face in surprise.

"You could have been killed." Her eyes were bright, her jaw clenched. "But I suppose you didn't consider that before diving into danger."

The leash on his temper frayed. "We both knew the danger going in. Am I glad the subject wasn't a better shot? Yeah. But our biggest problem at the moment is that he's still out there." The water was spilling from the shower onto the floor, but right now he didn't care.

"The agents were there. It was their job to protect us both. You took a needless risk." Her breath hitched once and with a jolt he realized that the brightness in her eyes came from a sheen of tears. "You could have been killed," she repeated fiercely.

Something in his chest softened and he reached out a hand, drew her inside the shower and pulled the door shut after her. "I wasn't. I'm fine." His gut clenched at the anguish on her face, and he recalled the last time he'd seen that emotion there. He'd been helpless to wipe it away eighteen months ago. He felt just as powerless now.

Her body was resistant as he drew her closer. "Two inches. That's all it would have taken. If your arm had been two inches farther back, the bullet would have entered right where the vest ends beneath your arm. It could have hit your heart. It could have…"

He pulled her close, laid her hand over his chest where he could feel his heart chugging like a locomotive. "It didn't. I'm right here, baby." Tucking her against his chest, he dipped his head, inhaling the fresh clean scent of her now-drenched hair. "I'm fine. We're going to be fine."

She was still for a moment and he could almost feel the internal struggle as she battled for her famed control. Could feel the instant she surrendered it, when she linked her arms around his waist and clung.

He held her like that for a moment, tightly enough to

deprive their lungs of oxygen. And he called himself every kind of fool for not seeing what had lurked behind her attitude, fueling the temper.

Cupping her face in his hands, he tipped it up to meet his. He slicked the water from her lips with the tip of his tongue and then delved deeper.

He tasted the welcome in her mouth, as well as a tinge of desperation that was easy to recognize. Her concern for him lit a flame in his chest that he'd thought long extinguished. Or maybe he'd been fooling himself on that front, too.

There was a message in her kiss, in her touch, that he was afraid to misinterpret. He'd never been especially good at translating her emotions. But this time, he vowed, his tongue gliding along hers, he'd get it right.

Her hands skated up his spine, sluicing the water off his shoulders. His mouth went to the cord of her neck and he scraped it with his teeth. An inch lower and he found the pulse at the base of her throat, throbbing like a caged wild thing. Heat licked through his veins.

His hands were fast and urgent when they pulled the soaked T-shirt over her head. Released the clasp of her bra. He let the water cascade over her breasts before capturing them in his hands. Things always seemed so clear when he could touch her like this. The passion between them at least had always been unclouded.

Pressing her back against the glass wall of the shower, he bent his head, took a nipple in his mouth and rolled it with his tongue. He heard the little gasp she made, felt the sting of her nails on his shoulders. A primitive flare of response fanned to life. He wanted her now, naked and wet and wild for him. He wanted to explore every inch of moist flesh with his mouth and then follow that exploration with his tongue.

But already there was no thought of slowing down, of

drawing this out. Not when her hands were gliding over his flesh, making teasing little forays closer and closer to where he was hard and straining.

His hands went to the clasp of her dark pants and fumbled, fingers unusually clumsy. He managed to unzip them, drag them over her hips, then halted when her fingers encircled him, doing a quick sensual dance up and down his shaft.

The air leeched from his lungs. Staggered and aroused, he could only stand there a moment, trying to haul in a gulp of oxygen. She could bring a man to his knees by touch alone. It took every bit of strength he had to withstand those wicked, knowing fingers and continue dragging her pants down her thighs, to temper his touch as he eased them over her own injuries.

When she stepped out of them he pulled her to him, a little rough, a little desperate. The water pouring over them echoed a pounding in his blood, in his chest. Wet flesh pressed against wet flesh. Steam curled around them, enveloping them in a heated cocoon of intimacy.

He parted the slick fold between her thighs to send a finger inside her, absorbing the buck of her hips against his. She was hot liquid fire around him, a tight dark promise that had the skin tightening at the base of his shaft in anticipation. The contrasts he found with her were gut-wrenchingly arousing.

There was the taste of her, exquisitely feminine, and the feel, wet curves over heat. The cool moist flesh of her shoulder, rounded and delicate. The velvet warmth inside her, clenching and releasing around his finger in a way that had reason receding.

Her hands stroked his sides, slid to his back, fingers flexing against muscle, trailing fire in their wake. Her touch torched his blood. He could feel it surging through his veins like a Thoroughbred straining toward the finish line.

With his free arm he brought her closer still against him, sealing their bodies together. Flesh to flesh. Curves to angles. Heat to heat. Her breasts flattened against his chest and he ducked his head to scoop up the rivulets of water dammed in her cleavage.

Her fingers went in search of him and he let his head fall back, awash in sensation. They might have been in danger for their lives hours ago, but he felt alive now. Incredibly so. Every breath he drew had to be battled in through clogged lungs. She stroked him urgently, urging him on, and he had to grit his teeth against the savage urge to mount her, ride her hard until they were both limp and satiated.

He wanted to believe that having her would lessen his desire. That he could whittle it away until there was nothing left but indifference. But all he had to do was drag his eyes open and watch the passion twist her expression to know his hope was doomed to fail.

Every gliding movement of her fingers sent a corresponding bolt of lust tightening low in his belly. She nipped at his shoulder, the tiny sting of pain shredding his control. He withdrew his finger from her and crowded her against the wall of the shower.

A man who couldn't take what he needed and walk away was a man truly caught. The truth danced at the graying hem of reason, taunting him. But all he wanted right now was to bury himself in her to the hilt, her velvety softness surrounding him with feminine heat. He wanted to plunge inside her until the pleasure exploded for both of them. And he wanted, quite desperately, for it to be enough.

His mouth on hers was rougher than he intended but she returned his kiss with a response that equaled his own. He used his good arm to lift her and she immediately locked her legs around his hips.

The position opened her to him, an invitation that was impossible to resist. His shaft nudged her slick folds as their mouths worked against each other, and she reached down with one hand to guide him. He sank into her with a hard lunge that drove the breath from both their bodies.

Dace stopped for a moment, tried to harness his flagging control. He wanted to watch her. Wanted to commit every change of expression to memory even as he began to thrust with a heavy insistent motion. But pleasure was crowding in, sensation slamming into sensation, making restraint impossible. His pace quickened until he was pounding into her, her heels digging into his hips, her nails biting into his shoulders. And when his release came, in a sudden powerful explosion, his mind was washed clean of every thought but of her.

The dressings had to be changed, of course. Somewhere during the tumultuous sex the plastic bag had worked down his arm. The bandages were soaked, as were those covering her wounds.

Dace sat on the edge of the tub, naked and docile as Jolie carefully cut a length of gauze. He lifted the dressing she'd applied, surveyed the wound critically. It was a nasty-looking crease but not a whole lot worse than the injury to Jolie's leg from that splintered wood, which she'd just re-covered. When he saw her watching him with false patience, he grinned and replaced the dressing with exaggerated care. She began wrapping the gauze around the thick dressing to hold it in place.

"I was wrong earlier."

"Call the news teams."

She should know better than to try sarcasm when she was still naked. He pinched her ass, and she glowered at him.

"You do have a good bedside manner. The best."

"And you have a woman standing over your naked body with scissors within reach. Be careful."

He grinned, stretching his legs out, lazily satisfied as he watched her work. "You can be *too* careful, you know. Caution is good when it keeps you alive. But not when it has you slamming the door every time you have a chance to be happy."

Her fingers slowed in their task. Because he was watching so closely, he saw her expression pale. Stubbornly, he plowed on. "We can't go back, you and me. But there's still something between us. Doesn't make sense for us to deny it."

She took more time than she needed to apply the adhesive tape to hold the gauze in place. When she lifted her gaze to meet his, he saw that her eyes were guarded. "Our mistake was thinking we could have more."

His good humor faded, foreboding tangling in his gut. "And what? We don't deserve more? Or you don't?"

When she would have ducked to pick up the materials she'd used, he grabbed her wrist, drew her upward to meet his gaze. "That's it, isn't it? You want to content yourself with bits and pieces of a life, because you aren't worthy of more? Who convinced you of that? That old bitch across town?"

"You couldn't possibly understand."

"Oh, I do." He gave a hard nod, a sheet of ice slicking over his skin. "I understand that you're going to let the past dictate the future. And not even your own past, but your mother's. That's a coward's way, Jolie. And you're not a coward."

Her smile was small and sad. "That's where you're wrong. I *am* a coward. Allowing you to tempt me to reach out for more, a chance at family, a real relationship…that was the bravest thing I ever did. I learned my lesson eighteen months ago. You should have, too."

Like a wraith, she slipped from his grasp and through the door, leaving him cold and alone with her words echoing and reechoing in his mind.

Jolie sat on the couch in the family room. The only light came from the muted television news. From the photos shown, she could tell they were recounting the scene at the memorial yet again. She made no move to change the volume. For once the case seemed of minor importance.

A sick knot of nerves tightened inside her when she recalled the look on Dace's face a couple hours ago. She knew she'd disappointed him yet again with her answer. But she was only protecting him—both of them—from more disappointment down the road. The hardest fall of all came from reaching too high. From wanting too much. Hadn't he learned that when Sammy died?

She hadn't heard a sound from upstairs in over an hour. Laying her forehead against her knees, Jolie found herself hoping that meant Dace was asleep. The shock to his system, followed by the heavy-duty pain medication, should do the job.

She wasn't so lucky.

Lifting her head, she stared blindly at the television, her vision burning. It was useless to wish things could be different. Useless to believe that anything she did or said could change the inevitable. Dace Recker was a man who believed he could have a normal life. And he deserved to find a normal woman who could share that dream with him.

Her cell rang and she turned her head slowly in the direction of the sound. For a moment she was tempted not to answer it. But the sound could wake Dace. And it could be news of the case. Or of Trixie.

But she didn't recognize the number on the screen. And

when she answered, it took her a moment to jerk herself back to the investigation.

"Detective Conrad? I know we promised to get back to you earlier, but the debriefing only recently broke up." The agent's familiar voice was brisk, impersonal. "I wanted to be the first to give you the news. We have the subject in custody."

Stunned, it took Jolie a moment to answer. "How? When?"

"I'll fill you in later. I'm afraid I have some unfortunate information for you. It seems while we were meeting, your mother disappeared."

A cold pool of fear spread in Jolie's chest. "Disappeared?" She turned to pace toward the couch and away again. "Where? She was left alone?"

Her questions went unanswered. "We've traced her as far as Bellamy Court." The park was the habitat of hookers and drug dealers after dark. "We can continue the search, but I thought I'd let you know, in case you'd like to join us. You may have more luck finding her than we will."

Jolie was already heading upstairs to change out of her oversize tee and boxer pajama shorts. "I'm coming with you."

"Not a problem." There was a burst of static, then the agent's voice sounded again. "…driving there myself. I'll swing by and pick you up in five minutes."

The call disconnected and Jolie did a quick change, a familiar sense of weariness filling her. This was her reality, and the contrast between it and what Dace was asking for couldn't be starker. She hesitated before going downstairs, deciding to strap on her weapon. Bellamy Court was notoriously unsafe, although it was the type of place where Trixie would feel at home.

When she got downstairs, she scribbled him a quick note in case he woke up and wondered about her whereabouts.

Looking out the window, she noted the dark sedan was

absent. Hawkins must have gotten the word that the feds had a suspect in hand. Lights speared down the street, and a car pulled to a stop outside the condo. Quietly, she locked the door and slipped outside, jogging to the discreet navy sedan.

Chapter 13

SAC Fenholt pulled away from the curb. "I expected to see Recker with you."

A stab of guilt pierced Jolie. "I thought being shot today was enough excitement. He deserves some rest." And he definitely didn't deserve another scene with Trixie. She wasn't his obligation, any more than Jolie was.

The woman checked oncoming traffic before turning the corner. "He can be updated about the break in the case tomorrow, I guess."

"Maybe you can give me the condensed version now."

"Chief Sanders passed along the link you and Recker made between the Marker brothers. He was rather insistent that we run a comparison between the DNA found at the bank scene and David Marker's DNA in the military database. We got a match. We pulled Adam Marker in on a BOLO bulletin."

Stunned, Jolie could only look at her. She and Dace had

thought the Marker connection was a strong lead. But she had no idea the feds would act on it so quickly. Sanders must have really muscled the follow-up. And it was apparent from Fenholt's grim voice that she wasn't happy about her team missing the link.

Questions swarmed her mind. "Has he been interrogated? How did he access the memorial site? How much of the banks' money can be recovered?"

"I wish I could answer those questions." Weariness sounded in the woman's voice. "But Marker lawyered up almost immediately. We're going to have to do this the hard way. If you don't mind, I'd like to switch the conversation to your mother. Does she have a cell? Are you able to call her?"

"No." Her earlier excitement deflated with the suddenness of a pricked balloon. "Trixie leads a high-risk lifestyle. I can imagine that Bellamy Court may be a former hangout of hers. Since the security detail began, I've contacted Agent Hart when I want to talk to her."

"So you have his number. Can I use your cell to call him?" The special agent gave her a wry smile. "To go along with everything else that could possibly go wrong today, my cell died right after I spoke to you."

"Sure." Jolie reached in her pocket and withdrew the cell phone. "Do you want me to bring up his number now?"

"If you would. Then I'll talk to him. See where the search stands."

Jolie accessed the number and handed it to the special agent. Fenholt was silent for a few seconds, then Hart must have answered. Without preamble the woman said, "Update me on the search. Have you found her yet?" She listened for a time then snapped, "Well, stay at it. We've got witnesses placing her in the park less than thirty minutes ago. You, Truman and Dawson spread out and comb it again. It's one woman. How hard can she be to find? I've got Conrad with me and we'll be there in five. I'll contact you again then."

Snapping the cell shut, she slid a glance to Jolie. "I'm going to keep your cell for the duration, if that's all right."

Giving a tired nod, Jolie leaned against the head rest, looking out the window. Four FBI agents were spending their evening looking for her wayward mother, and that was more than a little embarrassing. She should have expected that Trixie would make a run for it at the first opportunity. It was clear she chafed at the close observation she'd been under. Not for the first time Jolie wondered if she'd done her mother any favors by taking her in when Metro City Memorial Hospital had contacted her a few months earlier. Maybe Trixie was right. Did it really matter whether it was chemo, cancer or meth that got her in the end?

She drew in a breath. It mattered. To her, at least. She'd owed Trixie nothing, but something inside her had revolted at leaving the woman to her own devices while she died. It wasn't because she'd hoped to form a relationship with the woman before her death. She knew her too well for that. But a need for something—closure?—had her refusing to walk away when it would have been so much easier. Jolie's grandmother had been the only person in her life that had cared about her. She'd repay Gran in the only way she could. By not letting her wayward daughter die on the streets of Metro City.

Every sound in his bedroom seemed abnormally loud. Dace was aware of the click of the radio alarm counting each minute. The stirring of the blinds when the air conditioner turned on. The sound of his own breathing.

So he heard the door close downstairs. Assumed that one of the agents had returned. He knew Jolie had crept down there hours ago and hadn't returned upstairs. Which was why he was loath to go down himself.

When it came to Jolie, he was out of words.

There was a dagger of pain at the thought, and it wasn't in his arm. How did you convince a woman that she deserved happiness?

Especially since the one time she'd taken that chance, their world had caved in on top of them.

Dace opened his eyes, stared at the ceiling. He knew himself well. He was a man used to getting what he wanted once he studied all the angles and figured the best approach. But that tack didn't always work with people and especially not with a woman like Jolie. She was a mass of complications, and her own fears mounted a formidable obstacle. The mistake he'd made in the past was in not knowing her well enough and believing he could tear down those fears bit by bit.

He knew her better now. Well enough to know that she was the only one who could break free of her past and grab a chance for happiness. And recognizing that skewered him with a helpless feeling.

Scowling, he sat up and swung his legs over the side of the bed. He didn't hear voices downstairs. Matter of fact, he didn't hear anything. Maybe he'd dozed off a few minutes and Jolie had gone to bed earlier. At any rate, since he couldn't sleep he might as well go down and get Dawson or Truman to update him on the debriefing.

He pulled a pair of jeans on and padded downstairs. The TV was still on, muted, but he saw no one. Checking the front door, he found it locked. A quick check found no one downstairs. He turned and took the steps two at a time and opened Jolie's door. The couch hadn't been pulled out into a bed.

Meaning the sound he'd heard earlier was her leaving.

The first trickle of unease traced through him. She hadn't left for good. Her things were still upstairs. And she wasn't stupid enough to go out alone when they were still unsure of the status of the security detail.

But her phone had rung earlier. He'd heard it. Whatever conversation she'd had must have led to her taking off. He went upstairs to finish dressing, grabbed his cell and headed back down. It was then that he saw the note she'd left for him in her familiar neat handwriting.

He picked it up and flipped on the light to read it. His earlier unease intensified. Fenholt? Why would the SAC be involved in searching for Trixie?

Taking out his cell, he placed a call to Dawson and got his voice mail. Same with Truman. His heartbeat quickening, he put a call through to Jolie. A moment later he was invited to leave a message. What the hell?

He didn't have any of the other agents' numbers. But something about this didn't add up. Since no agent had returned to the condo, he assumed the security detail had been pulled for good. But what kind of operation made a decision like that without alerting the people who had been protected?

He tapped a beat on the edge of the counter with his index finger, thinking rapidly. Should he call Chief Sanders? Dace assumed the man would have been updated about the debriefing. Glancing at the clock, he decided against it. It was nearly eleven. And he had nothing to support this increasingly edgy feeling other than a missing addict and mounting suspicion.

The subject had accessed the memorial site. Not only accessed it, but had free rein to walk it, scattering gunpowder. To plant an IED. He'd infiltrated the perimeter with a weapon. Been seen in a police-issue vest. Probably had an ID.

Dace didn't necessarily believe the subject was law enforcement. But it sure as hell looked like he'd had LEO assistance. He stared at his cell phone, thinking furiously. His car was toast, thanks to the bomb at Jolie's place, and he hadn't had time to get a replacement. Even if he could contact any of the agents, whom could he trust?

A moment later, his decision made, he dialed another number. He was probably overreacting. Logic had him recognizing that. But the ice in his chest wasn't responding to reason. If there was a chance Jolie was walking into danger, he was damn well going after her. And he wasn't going in alone.

At one time Bellamy Court might have been considered the jewel of the city. But as Metro City had sprawled outward, it had been left to deteriorate, along with the rest of its inner-city neighborhood. Jolie had been in the area on calls before. No trained police officer would ever enter its confines alone at night.

The unmanicured vegetation was slowly encroaching on the grassy space. Only every third streetlamp or so was in working order. She waited next to a graffiti-marred statue as Fenholt contacted Hart again, a sense of disquiet filling her.

"Where? Contain the area. Conrad and I will approach from the south."

Fenholt flipped Jolie's phone shut. "Your mother is in the restroom in the center of the park. Think you can talk her out?"

Jolie fell into step as the agent began striding rapidly into the interior of the park. "I can handle it from here. Really, my missing mother is hardly deserving of four federal agents' time and energies."

"She is when she disappeared on our watch." Fenholt's disgust was evident in her tone. "Someone will answer for that, but for now, the least we can do is get her back safe and sound."

There was no more conversation after that. Jolie spent the few minutes as they walked into the wooded area contemplating just how she was going to get Trixie to leave with her. She was strongly tempted to cuff her and be done with it.

A building loomed ahead. The public restrooms. Jolie slowed, scanning the area. No one else was in sight. Her disquiet intensifying, her hand went to her weapon, an instinctive response.

Fenholt strode ahead, calling out, "Conrad! Come out!"

Jolie's flesh prickled. Seconds stretched. Something about the scene rang false. The place was too quiet. Where were the other agents?

She took a step back. Then another. Started to pull her weapon.

And then stopped mid-motion a moment later when a voice sounded behind her. "I don't think so, Detective Conrad. Drop it."

She whirled, weapon in hand, to face a man nearly hidden in the shadows. She couldn't make out his features, but it was easy enough to see the silhouette of the gun he held pointed at her. "Sorry to miss you this morning," he said, with heavy inflection. "But we can rectify that now."

"Hurry up, Marker." Fenholt strode over, weapon in hand, and disarmed Jolie. "I delivered her as promised. Get it over with so we can move on."

Comprehension slammed into her, too late to be of help. Dace had mentioned his concern of a law enforcement link. But never would Jolie have suspected the SAC herself.

But the pieces fit too neatly. She and Dace had noted a familiarity with LEO tactics when they'd negotiated the barricaded subject at the bank. And no one else had the authority to pull the agents from the security detail, leaving her and Dace vulnerable.

Throat tight, she said to Fenholt, "Where's my mother?"

"I have no idea." She heard the shrug in the woman's voice. "This was never about her. Once I pulled Hart into the debriefing and dropped the security detail, I imagine she took off. She's not really going to be your concern much longer."

"You were supposed to bring Recker, too," Marker said.

"I've got Conrad's cell phone. I can get him here. But first I want your word that this ends tonight. I took a hell of a risk 'losing' your brother's blood samples. Now you've stirred up such a crap storm with your revenge agenda that my career is going to play hell surviving it."

"That's where you're wrong, Gee. You aren't going to survive it." The muzzle flash accompanied by the sound of the silenced gun split the darkness. Fenholt crumpled. A split second later, Jolie was diving for the agent's weapon. Only to find Marker's weapon pressed against the back of her skull.

"Use your left hand. Pick it up by the barrel and toss it away."

Mind racing furiously, Jolie did as she was told. What had Fenholt done with Jolie's weapon? Tucked it in her waistband? Looking down at the body, she was unable to tell. But it made sense that she'd hang on to the weapon to dispose of later.

"Back away from the body. Now!" he barked harshly, when she was slow to move. "I guess I can always go after Recker once I'm done with you. Shouldn't be too hard since Gee was kind enough to get the federal babysitters removed."

Her breath strangled in her chest. Dace would be alone. Without protection. Probably asleep and vulnerable. The thought turned her veins to ice water. There was no way she was going to allow Marker out of this park alive to carry out his revenge on Dace. The man had to be stopped before anyone else died.

She rose, circling the agent's body to keep it between them. "So Fenholt was the brains of the bank heists. Convenient for you. I suppose she directed the investigation away from you and your record. Did she falsify your alibis, too? Manufacture evidence of a terrorist cell to misdirect the investigation?"

He moved, tracking her with the weapon. "She was useful for a while, I'll admit. Having a G-man—or in her case, woman—taking care of the details did come in handy. But she just couldn't understand that avenging David is more important than planning the next bank job. But I'll bet you understand, don't you, Conrad?"

"I understand more than you think." It was second nature to keep her breathing normal, her voice calm. She'd defused dozens of armed confrontations in HNT.

But none of those incidents had put her inches away from a loaded weapon. There was no full-response tactical back-up team to go in if she failed.

And if she failed, Marker was going for Dace.

"I'm the one who talked to David, remember? Actually, I spoke to him more than Detective Recker did."

"Shut the hell up," the man snarled. "Don't even mention his name to me. You got him killed!"

"He asked me to call him John," she said calmly. She continued to inch around the body, feeling for a weapon with the toe of her shoe. One chance was all she was going to get. It wasn't a matter of whether she could get to the weapon before Marker fired. She couldn't.

All she could hope for was that his first shot wasn't fatal.

"Don't you want to know what we talked about?" Tension was radiating off the man in waves. She knew just how tightly wound he was. But she didn't have time to establish rapport. She had to play the one card she had and hope it was the right one.

"Negotiators spend a long time talking to the barricaded subjects. Not just about the incident, but about what's going on in their mind." As that went, "John" hadn't been particularly forthcoming, but Marker didn't need to know that. "He spoke about you."

"You're lying. He was too well trained to give away any personal information."

"That's right." She stilled. Was that the weapon she felt beneath the woman's body? Wiggling her toes, she felt something hard. Her gun, or the cell phone? "He didn't mention you by name. But we talked about family meaning everything. He talked about having one person in particular whom he trusted. That was you, wasn't it? I figured a father. A brother."

"Half brother. You killed the only person in the world who meant anything to me. So you die for that. Can't say it isn't fair, can you, Conrad?"

Though she hadn't killed David, she didn't pursue that line of reasoning. Clearly to Marker any SWAT personnel who had been on scene was guilty. "He was practically the only one who visited you in prison, wasn't he? Even after he was in the military, he'd come on his leave to see you." She flexed her foot again. It was a weapon she felt under the fallen agent's body. She stilled. Waited for an opportunity.

"Guess Gee wasn't as good at covering my trail as she claimed," he said. "I know what you're trying to do. I studied some of that psychology crap in prison. It isn't going to work. I may not get the entire squad. I'll have to come back someday for Carter. She's the one who shot David, wasn't she? I'll want to plan something special for that bitch. But you and Recker die tonight."

She poised herself, waiting for an opportunity. Hoping he

was only half right. She might die tonight. But if she could get the weapon there was a chance that Marker would die with her.

The opportunity came from a different source than she expected. There was a flash of light and an explosion, shaking the ground beneath their feet. Jolie dove for the body, but she was disoriented by the detonation. She struggled to release the weapon from Fenholt's waistband. Gunfire split the night, and she rolled away, coming to a seated position with her weapon ready. Marker dropped to his knees, a stain spreading across his shirt. But he hadn't released his gun.

They stared at each other and time crawled to a stop. They fired simultaneously. The sounds echoed oddly. Or were there more shots? Hard to say. Hard to focus. Her head hit the ground. Strange. She was lying down. She had to get up. Had to get her weapon.

But her body didn't obey her fuzzy thoughts. Numbness was spreading from her chest, down her arm. The shadows were rushing in. The last thing she thought she saw was Dace. But that couldn't be. He was safely home in bed. His lips were moving, but she couldn't hear what he was saying. And then her vision blacked and she saw nothing at all.

"Then get that doctor in here, and get him in here now." If there had been something within reach Jolie would have dearly loved to hurl it, knocking that smirk off the nurse's lips. Although she suspected the woman wasn't a nurse at all but an undercover agent trained in specific methods of torture. "I'm not spending another night here."

Dace pushed the door open, surveying the scene. The nurse passed him, rolling her eyes. He grinned.

Noting the exchange, Jolie scowled. "You. Unless you've got my release orders, I have nothing to say to you."

"That's okay." He strolled in, looking remarkably fit in faded jeans and a well-worn gray tee. The sleeve didn't quite cover the dressing on his arm. "I've got plenty to say. You can just listen for a while."

Sulkily, she lay back in the bed. "Four days. Four. Whole. Days. This is ridiculous."

He cocked his head, studying her critically. "They say grouchiness is a sign of healing. You must be better. A *lot* better."

Ignoring the insult, she seized on his words. "Tell the doctor that. C'mon, Dace, I'd do it for you. You know I would."

"I don't know that," he countered, pulling a chair up to the side of her bed. "As a matter of fact, I seem to recall some not-so-polite remarks the last time I refused to spend the night in the hospital. Idiot was one." He looked up, as if trying to remember. "What was the other? Oh, yeah. Moron."

He was enjoying this too much. "Only means you should realize how desperate I am to get out of here."

"What I realize is how desperate I am to make sure you're well enough first. If it makes you feel any better, the doctor said possibly tomorrow."

She heaved a sigh, stared balefully at the ceiling. Tomorrow. He might as well have mentioned a month. A moment later, she turned her head to regard him. "How's Trixie?"

"The same." She winced at the careful reply. "Still at my place. Still, uh…colorful in her objections. My mother is with her now."

Horror rose. "You left Della with Trixie?"

"For all her surface charm, my mother could discipline a pack of wild orangutans. She'll be fine."

It was ridiculous to feel embarrassed knowing that an hour with Trixie would tell Della far more about Jolie's past than she'd ever revealed on her own. Ridiculous, because Dace's mother wasn't in her life anymore. Hadn't been for a long time.

"You've got to stop believing Trixie is a reflection on you. She has nothing to do with you, and that was her choice. You've given her far more power than she deserves over the years."

Shocked, she met his gaze, quickly looked away. His insight was disturbing. And it wasn't something she hadn't told herself many times. Some of the time she could even believe it.

A thought occurred and she returned her attention to him. "Are you and Langley okay with Sanders?"

She didn't miss his grimace. "He was…unhappy that I called Jack to pick me up and check out the park on our own. But Fenholt had made sure the agents would be stalled in that debriefing session most of the night. And he eventually admitted my suspicions would have been a tough sell had I called him or the lieutenant."

Meanwhile losing valuable time. A shudder worked through her. Langley had brought his equipment, and that had probably saved her life. The night-vision goggles had enabled the two to find them more quickly once they'd arrived, lights flashing, at the park. The flash-bang grenade had distracted Marker long enough for her to draw the gun from Fenholt's waistband. It hadn't saved her from Marker's shot, which had hit her in the shoulder.

But Dace's next shot had made sure Marker hadn't fired again.

"Sanders did say today that they've found a bank account in Fenholt's name in the Caymans with nearly ten million dollars in it. Guess that was supposed to tide her over when mandatory retirement hit. She was up to her neck in the thing." His voice was grim. "It was she who had busted Marker seventeen years ago. She probably approached him with the whole thing planned out once he was released. And she delivered for him, I'll say that. Lined up a job for him with an employer who would lie about his absences for a fee. Shifted the direction of the investigation whenever it got too close to him." His expression was sober. "It might have been Marker's idea to take us out, but with the lead we were pursuing, our deaths fit nicely into her agenda, too. Once the link was established between the Markers, things would unravel for her pretty quickly."

"She took a hell of a risk," Jolie murmured. "And all for money?"

"I agree. There are things a lot more worthwhile to take a risk on." Dace propped his hands on the side rail of the bed, regarding her steadily. "Things like a future. Love, even."

She gaped at him. She couldn't help it. She'd never heard him mention the word before. Would have run fast and far if he had.

"I spent a long time blaming you after you left." His voice was matter-of-fact. His gaze wasn't. It was intense. Hypnotic. Jolie couldn't have looked away if she wanted to. "Only recently did I realize that I shared some of that blame."

When she started to object, his voice overrode hers. "Maybe if we'd had more time before you got pregnant, we would have had a better foundation. Maybe you would have trusted me enough to let me in, just a little. Then I could have understood better what was going on in your head."

She tried to speak, found her throat raw. "You have no idea how much trust it took for me to stay with you. To have Sammy."

He gave a slow nod. "I think I do. Now, at least. But at the

time I thought it was enough that you stayed. I figured time
was on my side. That you'd see for yourself how good it could
be."

"But then Sammy died."

"And both of us closed down. You shouldered guilt that
wasn't yours to bear. I guess I did, too. It wasn't logical to
feel that I'd failed to protect my family. Took me a while to
get over that."

Shock made her voice urgent. "Sammy's death had nothing
to do with you."

"With either of us," he said meaningfully, and she fell
silent. Guilt wasn't logical and stemmed from one's own
deep-rooted fears. She had come to realize that. It hurt to
know that Dace had grappled with the same feelings, alone.

"If he had lived…" Her breath hitched once. "You can't
expect a child to be the glue that will hold two people
together. That's too much pressure."

"No, you can't. I was banking on time to get you to see
the truth, to recognize what was right in front of you." He
shook his head at her puzzled look. "Never thought I'd ever
be accused of subtlety." He reached down, drew one of her
hands through the opening between the rails to hold it in his.
"I knew I loved you long before Sammy was born. I remember the exact moment. You were sitting in the nursery
I'd just painted, rocking in the chair my mom had stripped
for us."

Her mind flashed back to the moment he was describing.
They hadn't wanted to know the sex of the baby so they'd
chosen apple green for the color. And as she'd sat and looked
at the room that was taking shape, she'd had the feeling she
was looking from afar. At someone else's life. One she'd
always been careful not to wish for.

His voice husky, he continued, "You had your hand over

your belly and this little smile on your face. And it was like getting kicked in the chest by a horse."

Swallowing hard, she said, "You never told me."

His thumb skated over the back of her hand. "I knew you'd run. Emotionally, at least. So I figured I'd wait until the baby was born and you saw how good it was."

"It was good," she recalled achingly. Sweet, if slightly alien, like the stolen snippets of someone else's life. "But that part of our lives is over. We can't go back."

"We can go forward."

Her heart stopped. Then it rushed forward with the speed of an oncoming locomotive as he continued. "I wanted to believe we were over. Thought we were. Until I opened the door of the van and saw you sitting at the table, my new partner. And it didn't take very long to realize we were never really over at all."

She looked down, was surprised to see her hand trembling in his. Even more surprised by the overwhelming sense of longing his words evoked.

He'd always had this power over her, a dangerous control. He could make her *want*. Not just physically, but an emotional longing that carried its own kind of risk. She could run from it. Had run for a long time. The question was whether she had the courage to stop running.

Her eyes met his. "I don't know how to do this. I'm not…" She shook her head. "I'm not a good risk in the love department. But in the park a few nights ago, I knew what I had to do. I was going for my gun trapped under Fenholt's body. I knew I couldn't beat him to the shot but I thought I might still have the chance to shoot if his first shot wasn't fatal." She saw his face blanch, damned herself for her lack of finesse. "I thought that was going to be my only chance to keep him from going for you. And I finally discovered what it meant to want to protect someone. I was willing to go to any lengths to keep you safe."

He raised her hand to his lips, pressed a kiss on it. "Does that mean you've forgiven me for my overprotective instincts?"

She finally understood what lay beneath the tendency. Finally recognized how emotion could overwhelm caution and good sense and lead to taking risks that a more cautious person would shy away from.

"It means," she said shakily, raising herself on one elbow, "that I'm willing to stick around and help you work on it."

She felt his smile on the lips he pressed against hers, and that pesky inner alarm stilled. She spent her life assessing threats and had finally realized the truth. Loving this man was a risk worth taking.

* * * * *

Don't miss Kylie Brant's next ALPHA SQUAD *book,*
Jack Langley's story,
TERMS OF ENGAGEMENT!
On sale January 2009,
only from Silhouette Romantic Suspense.

Here's a sneak peek at THE CEO'S CHRISTMAS PROPOSITION, the first in USA TODAY bestselling author Merline Lovelace's HOLIDAYS ABROAD trilogy coming in November 2008.

American Devon McShay is about to get the Christmas surprise of a lifetime when she meets her new client, sexy billionaire Caleb Logan, for the very first time.

Silhouette *Desire*

Available November 2008

Her breath whistled out in a sigh of relief when he exited Customs. Devon recognized him right away from the newspaper and magazine articles her friend and partner Sabrina had looked up during her frantic prep work.

Caleb John Logan, Jr. Thirty-one. Six-two. With jet-black hair, laser-blue eyes and a linebacker's shoulders under his charcoal-gray cashmere overcoat. His jaw-dropping good looks didn't score him any points with Devon. She'd learned the hard way not to trust handsome heartbreakers like Cal Logan.

But he was a client. An important one. And she was willing to give someone who'd served a hitch in the marines before earning a B.S. from the University of Oregon, an MBA from Stanford and his first million at the ripe old age of twenty-six the benefit of the doubt.

Right up until he spotted the hot-pink pashmina, that is.

Devon knew the flash of color was more visible than the

sign she held up with his name on it. So she wasn't surprised when Logan picked her out of the crowd and cut in her direction. She'd just plastered on her best businesswoman smile when he whipped an arm around her waist. The next moment she was sprawled against his cashmere-covered chest.

"Hello, brown eyes."

Swooping down, he covered her mouth with his.

Sheer astonishment kept Devon rooted to the spot for a few seconds while her mind whirled chaotically. Her first thought was that her client had downed a few too many drinks during the long flight. Her second, that he'd mistaken the kind of escort and consulting services her company provided. Her third shoved everything else out of her head.

The man could kiss!

His mouth moved over hers with a skill that ignited sparks at a half dozen flash points throughout her body. Devon hadn't experienced that kind of spontaneous combustion in a while. A *long* while.

The sparks were still popping when she pushed off his chest, only now they fueled a flush of anger.

"Do you always greet women you don't know with a lip-lock, Mr. Logan?"

A smile crinkled the skin at the corners of his eyes. "As a matter of fact, I don't. That was from Don."

"Huh?"

"He said he owed you one from New Year's Eve two years ago and made me promise to deliver it."

She stared up at him in total incomprehension. Logan hooked a brow and attempted to prompt a nonexistent memory.

"He abandoned you at the Waldorf. Five minutes before midnight. To deliver twins."

"I don't have a clue who or what you're…"

Understanding burst like a water balloon.

"Wait a sec. Are you talking about Sabrina's old boy-friend? Your buddy, who's now an ob-gyn doc?"

It was Logan's turn to look startled. He recovered faster than Devon had, though. His smile widened into a rueful grin.

"I take it you're not Sabrina Russo."

"No, Mr. Logan, I am *not.*"

* * * * *

Be sure to look for
THE CEO'S CHRISTMAS PROPOSITION
by Merline Lovelace.
Available in November 2008 wherever books are sold,
including most bookstores, supermarkets,
drugstores and discount stores.

nocturne™

ESCAPE THE CHILL OF WINTER WITH TWO SPECIAL STORIES FROM BESTSELLING AUTHORS

MICHELE HAUF

AND

VIVI ANNA

WINTER KISSED

In "A Kiss of Frost," photographer Kate Wilson experiences the icy kisses of Jal Frosti, but soon learns that this icy god has a deadly ulterior motive. Can Kate's love melt his heart?

In "Ice Bound," Dr. Darien Calder travels to the north island of Japan, where he discovers an icy goddess who is rumored to freeze doomed travelers. Darien is determined to melt her beautiful but frosty exterior and break her of the curse she carries...before it's too late.

Available November wherever books are sold.

REQUEST YOUR FREE BOOKS!

2 FREE NOVELS PLUS 2 FREE GIFTS!

Silhouette® Romantic

SUSPENSE

Sparked by Danger, Fueled by Passion!

YES! Please send me 2 FREE Silhouette® Romantic Suspense novels and my 2 FREE gifts (gifts are worth about $10). After receiving them, if I don't wish to receive any more books, I can return the shipping statement marked "cancel." If I don't cancel, I will receive 4 brand-new novels every month and be billed just $4.24 per book in the U.S. or $4.99 per book in Canada, plus 25¢ shipping and handling per book plus applicable taxes, if any*. That's a savings of at least 15% off the cover price! I understand that accepting the 2 free books and gifts places me under no obligation to buy anything. I can always return a shipment and cancel at any time. Even if I never buy another book from Silhouette, the two free books and gifts are mine to keep forever.

240 SDN EEX6   340 SDN EEYJ

Name	(PLEASE PRINT)	
Address		Apt. #
City	State/Prov.	Zip/Postal Code

Signature (if under 18, a parent or guardian must sign)

Mail to the **Silhouette Reader Service**:
IN U.S.A.: P.O. Box 1867, Buffalo, NY 14240-1867
IN CANADA: P.O. Box 609, Fort Erie, Ontario L2A 5X3

Not valid to current subscribers of Silhouette Romantic Suspense books.

Want to try two free books from another line?
Call 1-800-873-8635 or visit www.morefreebooks.com.

* Terms and prices subject to change without notice. N.Y. residents add applicable sales tax. Canadian residents will be charged applicable provincial taxes and GST. Offer not valid in Quebec. This offer is limited to one order per household. All orders subject to approval. Credit or debit balances in a customer's account(s) may be offset by any other outstanding balance owed by or to the customer. Please allow 4 to 6 weeks for delivery. Offer available while quantities last.

Your Privacy: Silhouette is committed to protecting your privacy. Our Privacy Policy is available online at www.eHarlequin.com or upon request from the Reader Service. From time to time we make our lists of customers available to reputable third parties who may have a product or service of interest to you. If you would prefer we not share your name and address, please check here. ☐

SRS08R

Romantic
SUSPENSE

**Sparked by Danger,
Fueled by Passion.**

Lindsay McKenna
Susan Grant

Mission: Christmas

Celebrate the holidays with a pair
of military heroines and their daring men
in two romantic, adventurous stories
from these bestselling authors.

Featuring:

"The Christmas Wild Bunch"
by *USA TODAY* bestselling author
Lindsay McKenna
and

"Snowbound with a Prince"
by *New York Times* bestselling author
Susan Grant

Available November wherever books are sold.

Silhouette®
Romantic
SUSPENSE

COMING NEXT MONTH